Made For You

By

Geneva St. James

2008

www.AlphaWorldPress.com

Printed in the United States of America

First Edition

Alpha World Press – "Our Message to the World" –

www.AlphaWorldPress.com

Library of Congress Control Number: **2008921888**

ISBN: 978-0-9767558-4-5

To Sayrita,

To a long history and
tales from the tax office.
Best always,

"I've been losing sleep,

You've been going cheap."

(Cher, song lyric)

Chapter 1 - Ice Cream

"Ring! . . . Ring! . . . RING!" Julie yelled at the telephone. Adrienne could have dialed right then and the signal was traveling down the wire and any second it was going to ring there. "Now. Now! Ring! Ring! RING!" She wanted to pulverize that beige, plastic box of electronics that was holding her life hostage. The dial face seemed to be laughing at her. "Ten, nine, eight, seven, six, five, four, three, two, one, RING!"

She pressed down firmly on the receiver to make sure that it wasn't off the hook. It wasn't. She stood looking at it thoughtfully for a few seconds and then picked it up and listened for the dial tone. Was it still in order? It was. She hung it back up. She took the towel off the clock and checked the time. (It was less distressing if she did not have to watch the unbearable minutes tick by.) Soon she would have to leave to meet Sarah, yet automatically her excuse program was activated and searching for one that would justify staying in. Had that bitch intercepted the message? Were they in bed right now?

Three hours before, after impulsively leaving the message, she had felt light-headed and optimistic. Julie had always had a great capacity for being exhilarated and sustained by even the remotest hope. She composed some dialogues in her head and practiced banter with herself, expecting the return call to interrupt her minutes later, but those minutes started stretching out. After the first hour, the insidious tinges of fear and doubt began to resurface.

After the second, anxiety triumphed and she began counting quarter hours, then ten-minute intervals, until finally she wasn't able to hold another thought outside of eight seconds. She closed her eyes and shook her head bitterly. "I never should have called."

Reluctantly, she put on her windbreaker, slowly packed her knapsack and took baby steps out the door.

* * * *

"No, no, no, no, yes, no, yes, yes, sisters?" Julie mumbled. "No, no, no." She stood at the top of the stairs counting women that she'd sleep with. It was always the same meeting place, at the top of the stairs in front of Dairy Queen. It was ideal for watching people as they filed up from the subway. Regular, stair-ascending speed treated her to a pleasingly voyeuristic, methodical, yet slightly disembodied anatomy display. A head with long, brown hair appears; a white arm carries a black purse; the foreplay of a navy skirt, but where are the legs? Show me the legs. Oh, disappointing, a little thick.

Sarah's round face and shoulders appeared. Her thin, short, black hair was parted on the side, and today her bangs were pasted to the right. Pasted to the left sometimes, or gelled straight up like a stiff paintbrush, combed back and held with plastic butterfly berets or prim bobby pins, hair-sprayed forward or lightly blow dried and tucked behind her ears,

Sarah's hair was not an afterthought. Julie could see the thick, padded, black straps of the knapsack hanging from her back. A purple, blue and white thin-striped tee shirt and jeans covered her short body. She was strong in the legs below the knees, chubby and soft above, all the way to her unremarkable breasts.

Grade Ten, Sarah had said, was when she began to hate her body, when she began to ignore it. She never asked for any of it, bleeding between the legs and having to walk by the boys in the hall. She hated being a girl, wanted to be a boy. If she were a boy, she told Julie, she would slump in her desk and get hard-ons in wrecked jeans.

"Hi," said Sarah when she saw Julie. "Am I late?"

"No, I'm early as usual."

"Oh, I thought I was late. I had to meet d.dee, and I was longer than I had planned. I had to proofread her rebuttal of the dildo castration performance."

"How exactly does one 'rebut' a performance? What's her theme again this year? No wait . . . trans-something . . . portation, right? No one said these words twenty years ago."

"That's the problem."

"I think the problem's there's only so much you can blame on the imperialist capitalists, Sarah. Your girlfriend seems to employ two major strategies to fight all the injustice in the world. One; sit at her computer all day forwarding supposedly worthy emails; and two, write rebuttals."

"She does more than that."

"Yeah, she *tells* everyone how concerned she is about others, but just ends up talking about herself. 'Who am I? Where do I fit in? What's my identity? I'm so oppressed.' She doesn't know what oppression really is,

Sarah. Has she been owned? It's easy to spout slogans when you've got a clean bed, clean water, and penicillin if you need it. Seriously, I cannot understand half of what she says these days. She was much easier to understand three years ago. She uses made-up words that aren't even in the dictionary."

"*Astronaut* wasn't in the dictionary at one time too, you know."

"Let me know when a Pisces, vegetarian . . . What's the rest of it? Anarchist, pacifist, lesbian feminist with separatist tendencies lands on Mars, will ya?"

They walked out of the mall and into the wind where grit and paper whipped around viciously. Long, accordion-style Vancouver buses lined both sides of the street, making it claustrophobically narrow. They darted out between two of them and crossed in the middle of the block.

"Anyway, she wants to see if she can get the rebuttal published in *LaZine*," said Sarah.

"She's a writer, too."

"She *is*."

"You mean at that software company where she works full-time. Oh yes, I forgot. Isn't she overseeing that project with the ESL turtles?"

"Pandas. And for your information, endearing characters accompanying educational material have been phenomenally successful worldwide. Or perhaps you're too good for *Sesame Street*. Learning can be fun. You can reach children who may not be reachable otherwise. It's obvious that you are ignorant of the careful and extensive research that went into the choice of pandas. And she has written some good poems, too."

"Whatever you say, Sarah. Whatever you say."

"I'm going to let this drop because all experts say that heightened antagonism is an unavoidable side effect for people in your situation. Hey, do you mind if we stop off at Connections so I can check my e-mail?

"Sure, no problem."

"Something's driving me crazy."

"You, too? Wait till you hear about the clothes. What's up?"

"Remember when I went to Mexico?"

"Yeah."

"Well, I didn't take the right settings to check my e-mail from there, so I opened up a temporary account, but now I can't remember the password. I have this feeling that there are some lingering messages at that account."

"Don't those temporary accounts expire after ten days or something?"

"Not if you use it again within those ten days, and I did. Even if they're not important, I have to read them."

"Didn't you write it down somewhere?"

"Of course, but I can't remember where I put it."

"Saraaaaaah. You're usually good with stuff like that."

Sarah was good with stuff like that. She made not only shopping lists, but activity lists, guest lists, goal lists, and pros and cons lists. She jotted notes on the calendar for reminders, and she had never lost the original tiny scrap of paper on which she had encoded her PIN numbers.

"I know, but it was so easy . . . ."

"Obviously not. Did you check every corner of your wallet?"

"Yes."

"Your knapsack, every zipper?"

"Yes. It was so easy, something like 'Sarahmex' or 'Sarahinmex' or 'Sarahinmexi', maybe even 'Mexisarah'. Hey, maybe it was 'Tequila'. Now I'm getting all confused. I tried so many combinations last time that it shut down on me. I want to try just one more time. 'Sarahinmex'."

They walked into Connections. Julie watched over Sarah's shoulder as she sat in the black office chair and typed smoothly over the keyboard. "Damn it. Try again. Sarahinmex. Sarinmex. Samex."

"You got it!"

The screen Sarah had been typing on dissolved and opened up onto the inbox of an e-mail program.

"Seventeen messages? Oh my god!" whispered Sarah. "This isn't my account, Julie. This is someone else's account!"

"No way!"

"Way. Oh my god. This can happen. This can happen? I am not reading anything. I'm gonna close it."

"Wait a minute, Sarah," said Julie as she looked around stealthily to see if anyone was watching. "Come on. Just click on the first message."

"No."

Julie put her hand over Sarah's and pressed. "There. Just like that. That's right."

Mom and Dad were here for their vacation, and that turned out to be surprisingly bearable, the mail began. *Anyway, I have something to tell you! It's going to be a bit of a surprise I'm sure, but I want you to know that I have been seeing Ian since Christmas and things are progressing nicely. It's probably more surprising to me . . .*

"Julie, stop. Stop!"

"What are the odds of this?"

"Julie, I want to close it. It's just like reading someone else's mail."

"I know!"

"Julie, it's against the law."

"Not necessarily, Sarah. Internet law is a whole new bag of tricks. What may be illegal in one country is legal in another, and therefore many laws are not applicable within this international forum. It's an international waters or airspace kind of issue. It's a new frontier. Trial and error."

"This is error! It's not morally right to read other people's mail, Julie," Sarah whispered. "Everyone knows that." She kept looking over her shoulder to make sure that no one was coming near the cubicle.

"Come on. Let's try something. We are unlikely to get this chance ever again. Hit Reply."

"What?"

"Hit Reply."

"No."

"Come on."

"Why?"

"Trust me."

"No."

Julie leaned over and hit the button. She nudged Sarah over, took control of the keyboard and typed hurriedly, *Ian? You're seeing Ian? I am sorry, but I think you should know that I have some issues with Ian. However, it would be unfair to intrude upon your happiness right now by digging up the past. We can have a chat later. I do wish the best for the both of you. I sincerely hope it works out.* Julie then flashed Sarah an enormous smile and, with a defiant, staccato tap, hit the Send button.

"I can't believe you," growled Sarah. "Let's get outta here."

They scurried out the door and headed to Lavender's. The wind blew grit into their faces and they put their heads down, squeezed their eyes shut and scooted down the sidewalk.

It had been an unusually dry, dusty spring and summer for the West Coast. The sky had remained a majestic light blue with only the occasional non-threatening thin, white clouds sailing quickly over and out of the city. Every day the sun beamed benevolently on the neat green lawns and overflowing gardens, where merely observing the act of watering flooded the senses. Like a hypnotist's chain, sprinklers shot their entrancing, thin spouts back and forth, back and forth, methodically soaking everything into dazzling green. Thick, luscious blossoms expanded and then released the delicate drops that had been resting temporarily upon them.

Once at Lavender's, Julie and Sarah eased into a large, comfortable booth covered in slippery plum vinyl. The three booths along the wide front windows were the only part of Lavender's that suggested the service industry. A lot of money had been spent making the coffee shop feel as casual as a country get-away family room.

Up two steps from the booths, was a spacious raised area with six square wooden tables and accompanying chairs with more thick, plum vinyl-padded seats. Against one railing was an old, dark green, plush sofa. In front of the sofa was a low, glass and wood coffee table scattered with newspapers and magazines. Lining the dark, wood wall opposite the railing were exhibitions of local artists, a bulletin board plastered with notices, and a floor-to-ceiling pine bookcase, jammed with books. Sarah theorized that people relaxed at Lavender's and, when they relaxed, they became incautious. Therefore, it was a good place to bring prospective mates. Even Sarah and Julie's hairdresser, Jennifer, agreed. She talked about the atmosphere being the same as her quiet, private salon on the top floor of the old house. "When I moved there from the big salon, you would not *believe* what was confessed to me! Everyone was suddenly having an affair. I'm talking the mousy, shy ones! People open up in places like this."

Julie and Sarah could sit for hours in Lavender's discussing, analyzing, and repeating the same themes via not wildly varying current configurations of plot. "You two talk about nothing!" d.dee had once raged, yet their conversation was rarely stale, more often motivating and cathartic.

"So, what happened with the clothes?" asked Sarah.

Julie had been waiting for Sarah to turn the conversation to her, to what *she* wanted to talk about. These days for Julie, talk with friends was rarely a volley anymore. When she wasn't weeping or raging, she communicated mainly in pained, stifled monologues. She remembered symbiotic conversation only as a characteristic of long ago sweet beginnings of love affairs. "What musical instruments did you play as a child?" she had inquired as she looked searchingly, deep into Adrienne's eyes. She had more. "If I were ice cream, what flavour would I be and how would you eat me?" Adrienne had played that game, too. "If you could be any animal . . . ." Now, Julie was on listening automatic pilot where she dished out pre-programmed replies until it was her turn to speak.

"I stuffed them into a black garbage bag, and Tracey the Flunky came to pick them up. Cowards. Too afraid to show their faces."

"Oh, I figured that. You didn't really expect Adrienne to come, did you, Jules? It's too early. It's only been two and a half weeks. She's not going to come near you."

"Why? What are they afraid of? I know everything about them. I'm not going to do anything, won't come down to their level. I just want the cowards to face me instead of sneaking around the bushes. Like snakes. They're the ones who are poisonous, not me."

"Meagan told Colleen that you sounded berserk on the phone, Julie. Colleen said Meagan said she was afraid that you'd really kill her."

"Kill her? Oh, right. She's just trying to deflect scrutiny so she won't look so bad. Just because I said it doesn't mean I would actually do it. I was understandably upset."

"I know you wouldn't really, Jules, but I wouldn't trust anyone in this situation. Why do you think they call them 'crimes of passion' anyway?" Sarah hesitated cautiously here and then added, "I hear that they are going to go to Goldfinger on Saturday to make their debut as a legitimate couple."

"Legitimate! You cannot be legitimate when you start out how they did! They have nerve, though; they are *not* legitimate, Sarah."

"I might stop by there on my way home from class," continued Sarah quickly in hopes that Julie would be pacified by distraction. "My class is going really well, by the way. We're studying *The Handmaid's Tale* right now. Atwood is such a fine writer. She employs the most exquisite use of the semicolon that I have ever seen."

"Oh."

"It's so refreshing to read women and not the stuffy, pompous, macho curriculum that we had forced on us all those years. Hemingway accused women of being sentimental and writing only about love. Well, men could be said to write about only their first blowjobs and their various masturbation techniques."

"You sound like d.dee."

"It's my opinion."

"I should go, too."

"I don't think it's a good idea, Jules."

Julie twirled her empty cup like a top. "Maybe you are right, but I have to see Adrienne. When is she going to face me?"

"She faced you and you threw a magazine at her."

"I broke down and called her today. She didn't call back. What does she see in her? What's so great about Meagan anyway?"

"Nothing, Jules, but remember I told you that she's in film. It's a great seducer."

"I'd hardly say *in film*. She's a mature film student who has done a few overrated assignments. It's not Cannes here. She works in a tanning salon, Sarah. Is she even still in school?"

"I don't know."

"The film I saw at the festival was all grainy with bad sound, but she was still being treated like she was a genius. Here's the plot: There's a girl crying; we don't know why. Let's go out on a limb and say it's from a broken heart. She's sitting on the edge of a bed in a camisole staring dreamily into space. Original. Suddenly the bed is no longer a suitable place for this action, so now she's in the bathroom and, ohmygod, there's a villain behind her! We can see his face in, you guessed it, the medicine cabinet mirror. He's got a knife, not a gun; a knife! Can't blow her head off or scene's done. What story is this, Sarah? Is there no other scene available?"

"I haven't seen her work, so I can't comment."

"I can comment. You haven't missed anything. She's out of her league in the big pond. Hell, I should go into film and live off undeserved compliments and wreck other people's lives, too. It's falsely glamorous banality, Sarah."

"Why did you go then?"

"I thought that I might see a good film. I won't make that mistake again. There were Meagan and her minions handing out cheap leaflets that looked like they'd been mimeographed in the backroom of an underground, under-funded, 1960's Communist movement. And I thought all of this *before* she stole Adrienne."

"People can't be stolen."

"Whose side are you on anyway? Am I the only one who sees that she's all second-rate schemes? Why do people follow her? And when she's selfish and pushy, you say that we have to expect and tolerate behaviour like that because she's *in film.* Her remote artistic ability does not justify her arrogance, and esoteric is not synonymous with genius, you know."

"Julie, you're biased. All the relationship experts have you pigeonholed, by the way. Your reactions are textbook. I don't know her, but I think she has some talent."

"Marginal, believe me. You know what she once did with the rent money that Lisa gave her?"

"You told me already."

Sarah was thirteen years familiar with the ranting and she knew what to do: leave no room for segue. Just shut up and let Julie talk herself out.

"Sarah?"

"What?"

"I'm gonna get Adrienne back."

Chapter 2 - Center of Your Universe

One swift blow to the head with the ashtray is all it takes, recalls Julie. After I seduce her or let her *think* that she seduces me. I do it during pillow talk.

Julie is desperately trying to remember all of the details of her recurring dream. The seduction has to be flawless. It has to be flawless because I am up against an expert: Meagan. It is Meagan's role, and it never varies. She can alternate between fashionably feminine or casually dashing; she can embroider glory or misfortune, but she is always the irresistible seductress. But what she doesn't know is that this is precisely her weakest link.

Okay, Meagan returns from the bathroom. She's receptive and relaxed, even a little smug. She's doing up my robe that she found hanging on the back of the bathroom door. (Hope you don't mind if I wear this.) She stretches out on her stomach next to me on the bed. "You know, I've always wanted you," she says. "In a way . . . ." and she pauses here and slips her left hand inside her right one and strokes her palm gently and looks for all the world like she can't get enough of listening to her own voice, "more than Adrienne."

I light a cigarette and take a Bette Davis drag. I think about earlier when she told me how women invariably compete to light her cigarettes.

Did I know how many would jump for that chance? I'm jumping too, but it's my stomach with tingling chills. She's now propping her head in her hands and smiling into the pillow. Crack! Down comes the clay ashtray I made in 8th grade Industrial Arts class. The white flannel sheets start to soak crimson.

What happens after that? What do I do with the body? Am I in a hurry? Do I get caught? I need the end of the dream before I make my move. Have to go through the notebook again, maybe it was in there and I just missed it.

Julie thought it was helpful that she had started writing down her dreams about a year ago. *Dreams* she had printed on the subject line of a notebook cover, just as she would have printed *Math* or *French* years ago in school.

The experts said to write them down, but it really was not as simple as that. Ironically, the apathy produced during deep sleep was tougher to battle than any classroom boredom. *Open your eyes and write it down. Open your eyes. No, no, I'll remember in the morning.*

If there was even a hint of Adrienne being slightly awake, Julie would unknot the tangled sheets and roll over close and desperate in the dark, shaking her gently and entreating her to help.

"Adrienne . . . Adrienne."

"Mmmmmm."

"Adrienne," Julie whispered. "Remember the ace of spades was getting longer, and Dad was trying to sway the gondola cables."

"Mmmmm, what? Julie, move over."

Another impediment was eyesight. Julie needed to buy glasses. Without her contact lenses, Julie had to hold the alarm clock up to her nose. When she awoke during the night and scrawled something down, it was often illegible the next day. If it were a note to remind herself to buy milk or take in some drycleaning, then she probably would have been able to decipher it. But it was difficult to decipher the dream.

"Moondog did what? Can you read this word, Adrienne?"

The Moondog dream had produced their first significant fight; the first escalation from mild arguing to hurled accusations, door slamming and grinding emotion. It was always arrestingly painful and magnified, that first imperfection in the new, wondrous love that had been sustaining the two of them in their *own* world. A perfect surface suddenly blemished, like dirty, smudged footprints on a just-mopped floor, or urine in the fresh snow; that first venomous fight could be a silent, slow, sinister virus that infected the relationship with irreversible, slow poison.

"Did I say anything to you last night? Do you remember anything?" she asked as she absent-mindedly wagged her spoon up and down in Adrienne's direction.

"I don't remember," said Adrienne flatly.

"Are you sure?"

"I'm sure, Julie. And don't fling milk at me. Watch what you're doing."

Julie was so engrossed in deciphering that she did not notice the tone in her lover's voice.

"Nothing? 'Moondog' ring a bell?"

"No, Julie. 'Moondog' does not ring a bell." Adrienne took a glass from the cupboard and slammed it shut. She opened the refrigerator and took out the orange juice. "The old milk is still in here," she said accusingly. "Why did you start the new milk when the old milk isn't finished yet?"

"I just don't like using the last little bit. I like opening new ones. You know that."

"So you thought you'd leave the dirty work for me."

"I didn't think it bothered you. You should have said something before. Sorry. Please, could you just take a look at this a sec? Can you make out that word after 'did'?"

Sullenly, Adrienne picked up the notebook, glanced at it and then threw it back down on the table. "I can't read that, Julie. *How* can I read that scrawl? And I'm supposed to know what a 'Moondog' is?"

Julie was now interrupted sufficiently to begin absorbing Adrienne's irritation. "It's a dog," Julie said softly and incredulously. She looked at Adrienne with a look of hurt disbelief, like that of a child who had for the first time disappointed a previously adoring adult.

"How am I supposed to read that?" she snapped back.

"Well, you don't have to get so cross. I ask you because you know my mind like other people don't." She looked up at Adrienne again briefly and then down at her cereal and pursed her lips. "Well, I am sorry. I just thought that you might be able to figure it out. Like remember when I guessed your password? Maybe it floated into your dreams and you held on to it. I don't know. Forgive me. I can see that I've made a big mistake."

"I don't know what you write down your stupid dreams for anyway."

"They're not stupid. I told you already. They give you insight into your life."

"Indecipherable insight."

"Okay, fine then!" Julie slapped her pen down on top of the notebook. "I won't ask you anymore, okay? Just forget about ever helping me again. I'll keep my dreams to myself from now on." She was crying full force now. "I'm getting ready for work. If you're not in love with me anymore, why don't you just come right out and say it? Have a nice day," she said and stormed out of the kitchen.

After another round that evening, Julie slept in the spare room. She actually *spent the night* in the spare room since sleep was nowhere evident as she lay wide awake on the stiff bed under the afghan her mother had knitted. She passed an anxious, longing, fitful night, keenly waiting for the sound of footsteps and a warm, familiar body, contrite and on fire to slide in beside her. But Adrienne did not come and she had to swallow that resentful concession and then try to make herself fall asleep as quickly as possible.

First she tried to make her mind a blank space like she'd read about; concentrate on pushing all thoughts out as soon as they come in. You want a blank space; a clean slate, a dark screen. Erase, erase, erase. You will think about nothing. You will think about nothing. You will concentrate on a pinpoint of light in this black, blank space. On Tuesday at lunch . . . NO! Zap it outta there! She tried starting at the tips of her toes and working her way up, mentally massaging herself to sleep, but gave up mid-thigh. She'd try anything. One sheep, two sheep, three sheep; this is ridiculous. Toss, toss, toss; turn, turn, turn. Fights. So many stupid fights born of irritation rather than substance and then stubbornly clung to as a matter of misguided principle.

After ignoring each other obstinately for thirty-four hours, they made up the next night. Oh god, it was ecstasy, the reunion with that silent, hot body; trembling, kissing, crying as tentative and gentle as if they were the Earth's only survivors, searching each other to suture the wounds. It had been their worst fight to date, and Julie wondered if it were true, that old saying that sometimes couples fought just to enjoy sweet reconciliation.

All day Julie would anticipate crawling into bed next to Adrienne after they had started living together. Bed was more than sex. *I knew her dreams. She lay beside me when she had them.*

"Where am I going to bed every night? I'm going to bed with you, Julie. Why can't you remember that? Your anxiety is strangling our love."

That's what Adrienne had said. *You strangled me.* One year, ten months, nine days and that was all? *You strangled me?*

"Julie, it started when we were dating, before we were dating, actually. If I didn't return your e-mail soon enough, you'd go crazy. If I didn't acknowledge your letters, you'd think that I had read something in them that had made me suddenly despise you, or you'd think that you had offended me with choice of adjective. If I didn't call back immediately, I was out on a spectacular date, of course better than anything you could ever dream up in a million years. Or I could also be pretending that I wasn't home, or I was having sex with someone else, maybe two people, that very second. Great sex, too. Hot, kinky, transfusion sex definitely superior to what you could ever muster. No matter how many times I told you not to think like that, you did anyway. Providing constant reassurance to a partner is not romantic, Julie."

"I couldn't help it. I can't help it. I just want to be the center of your universe, Adrienne. Why don't you want to be the center of *my* universe?"

"Because that's not a partnership, Julie. It's a dominating and draining babysitting job."

"Babysitting! Now I am offended."

"You're throughout my universe, Julie, but you're not the single focus. You're huge, but you're not the center. I am sorry. I can't make only one person the center. What happens if you die? I have to rely on myself. Your way is limiting and suffocating."

"I'm not going to die."

"Julie, I'm drained. That's all."

"Are you implying that I'm high maintenance?"

"That's an understatement."

"That hurts, Adrienne. You're lumping me in with the likes of d.dee on the basis of that one category of insecurity? It's universal to relationships, not just ours. It's minor compared to the problems other couples have. You're neglecting all my good points. If you had just *responded* to the e-mails, then I'd have been all right. Tell me I won't hear from you for a week. Fine. You just had to tell me something. Why is it a weakness to crave confirmation? You say you want passion, well passion is not even and controlled; it's flawed and messy, like me. It was just when you didn't answer that I panicked. A five-word e-mail would have sufficed. 'Sorry. Busy. Talk next week' and I would have been fine. That's not a huge effort, Adrienne. How was I supposed to know what was going on? Were you out of town? Had there been an accident? Were you sick? What does it take, twenty seconds? You could even use all capitals; scream it at me. Why is it too much to ask? My friends are too lazy to write subject lines, can't I ask for more than that from someone I'm dating, from someone I am about to fall in love with?"

"I shouldn't have to do that if I had told you once already not to always imagine the worst. You should have believed that I really liked you.

All the time that we've been living together, it's like you never believed that I truly loved you and wanted to be here. You've treated it like an accident, a trap."

"This is all in the past, Adrienne. Why are you bringing it up now?"

"It continues into the future, Julie. It's the same pattern."

"What pattern? For example?"

"I know that you read my mail, go into my things looking for some kind of betrayal."

"*You* used to read your letters to me anyway. That's human nature, not a personality defect, Adrienne. Practically every great novel in history has somebody steaming open an envelope in it. You ask anyone if they haven't read their partners' letters."

"You cling, Julie. You're a dweller, always thinking that I'm just about to walk out the door on you."

"Well, you are right now, aren't you? Isn't that what this is all leading up to?"

"*You drove* me out, Julie."

"What are you saying? I would never drive you out, Adrienne. I love you. What about all the good things? What about all the good things?"

Numbness rose upwards from Julie's stomach. "Is it someone else?" It was not a spontaneous question. She had not thought it and then deliberately asked it right then. It has been formulated long ago and merely laid dormant. It was as predictable and involuntary as the wax on a candle melting down to a stub.

"No."

"Who is it?"

"No one. I'm just tired of taking care of you. That's all."

"You said . . . you said that you loved me unconditionally."

"Things have changed."

"How? How have they changed? I haven't changed. You said that I could lean on you."

"You were too heavy."

"What about everything you said? What about everything you said! All those promises you made?" Julie was trying to control the frantic escalation in the tone of her voice. Maybe if she could control that, then she could push this situation down; it wouldn't be real.

"There are no guarantees in love."

"You're profound."

"Here's another one, then: there are no guarantees in life or love."

"So, they were all just lies."

"I meant them at the time."

"But you don't mean them now, so they were all just lies!"

"I meant them then," said Adrienne as her voice rose to match Julie's.

"Don't you see? If you meant them then, it means that they were all just lies!" screamed Julie.

"All right. If that's what you want to hear. They were all just lies."

Julie threw a *National Geographic* at Adrienne's head. "Get the fuck out and never let me see you again!"

It didn't take long for Julie to find out that Adrienne was with Meagan. Meagan's ex, Lisa, who still held a considerable grudge, told Colleen, who told d.dee, who told Sarah, who told Julie. Sarah debated how to tell Julie. There was no better way. She decided to call.

"Hi. Whatcha doing?" Sarah had asked.

"Nothing. Just had a bath. What are you doing?"

"Nothing. I'm just . . . ummmm, what *am* I doing?"

"You sound funny. Is something wrong?"

"No, why?"

"I don't know. You just called to say that you don't know what you're doing? OH! Is it about Adrienne? What is it, Sarah? Say it, Sarah! Say it!"

"Okay, Jules, I have something to tell you, and I need you to remain calm."

"I will. Tell me!"

"Jules, she's with Meagan."

"That fucking bitch."

* * * *

Four months ago, Julie had organized a dinner and advertised it in the personals of one of the weekly gay papers. Turnout had been extremely successful with almost fifty women attending, and it had been the last time that she had seen Meagan. She had booked an Italian restaurant. It seemed to her one of the easiest choices with which to accommodate and minimize the demands of the inevitable vegetarians that would surely be present. One could always fall back on good ol' vegetarian pizza, she reasoned. Julie was reluctantly tolerant and hugely suspicious of vegetarians, vegetarian lesbians in particular.

"Why are there so many of you in the community, Sarah?" she often asked.

"I don't know."

"I'm talking ratio wise. It's staggering as, say, compared to vegetarian engineers or vegetarian dental hygienists."

"You're mixing up the categories."

"You know what I am trying to say. Hey, maybe now I know what d.dee means by all her constructed identity stuff. It's almost like a prerequisite these days, isn't it? Boy, how many times have I seen that scene where you act like you've been poisoned if you bite a teeny bacon bit? How come most of you'll eat chicken and fish and pretend it's not meat?"

"It's mainly red meat we stay away from."

"What's the difference, red meat, white meat, blue meat? And then there is the romantic boycott; the proclamation that you can't possibly date anyone that ate meat, anyone that didn't share your values. Hasn't d.dee switched back and forth a couple of times now?"

"She's entitled to phases. She's pretty firm now, though."

"Pretty firm. How do you wobble on an inviolate conviction?"

"People can change."

"That's true. Do you know any good vegetarian cooks, Sarah? No offense, but you certainly aren't. I've never met one."

"d.dee's a good cook."

Julie waited for the punchline. When it didn't arrive she said, "I'm sorry, Sarah, but she always buys the cheapest ingredients that she can find, and truly, the praise is in excess. You remember that time at Colleen's parents' place when she came back with six of those white, mystery vegetables? Nobody knew what they were. She just bought them because they were cheap, and absolutely inedible I might add."

"Okay, Julie."

"I can't stomach the name-dropping, either, like it somehow enhances her character. You know, Drew Barrymore is a vegan and ...."

"That's *enough*, Julie."

"George Bernard Shaw said he'd never eat his friends the animals ...."

"Drop it, Julie!"

"Why does she never mention Hitler? Isn't he one of the most famous vegetarians of all? I hope you realize that it is all the same underpinnings. You know what I'm gonna do? I'm gonna apply for a research grant to study the possible link between lesbian vegetarians and severe personality disorders. I am not kidding."

At the dinner, Adrienne, Julie, Sarah, and d.dee had sat at the middle table. Julie was now struggling to recall any interaction between Adrienne and Meagan that evening. She couldn't. There was nothing. Meagan was two tables away, and Julie could not now recall Adrienne even looking in that direction. This is because Adrienne was burning with premature lust and guilt and willing herself not to look over there. Like a diver dragging the bottom of a lake for a body, Julie repeatedly dragged all through her available memory trying to kickstart her unconscious. The net kept coming up empty.

"Can anyone recommend a wine?" Colleen had asked. "Chilean wine," said Meagan. "Definitely Chilean."

"Which one? There are a few here."

"Anything Chilean is popular right now. Just choose one."

"Hey, Meagan," said Colleen. "Did you hear that Michelle just got a job at Easy Listening CFMQ?"

"Yeah, I know. I heard part of her program the other morning. She won't last long. She's too A.M."

The phone rang and interrupted Julie's unrelenting attempt to recall the dinner and the ashtray dream. "Hi. Whatcha doing?" asked Sarah.

"Not much. Just had a bath."

"Julie . . . ."

"What?"

"At the height of her depression, Christina Onassis had three baths a day. You're up to two."

"What are you talking about? I'm fine. They relax me."

"I'm worried about you, and you're listening to that tape again. I can hear it in the background. Why do you torture yourself? Throw it in the garbage."

"I *need* to listen to it."

"I want that tape, Julie. I want you to give it to me next time I'm over. Promise?"

"You know what I really like best about the tape, Sarah?"

"Promise?"

"You know what I like best?"

"No, what?"

"I love the way that it cuts off at the end, three-quarters of the way through the last song. You've gotta be really skillful to engineer something like that. You know what I'm sure that Meagan did?"

"I want it."

"I might give it to you if you listen. Now you know what I'm sure that she did?"

"No, what?"

"Remember how she was a volunteer for Welcome Wagon?"

"Yeah."

"Well, she obviously did that just to meet foreign women, to get an exotic girlfriend. At least get first crack at them anyway when they were vulnerable. There is no way that she would greet immigrants and help them adapt to North American life if there wasn't some benefit in it for her."

"Are you getting out at all? Going to the gym or getting any exercise at all?"

"Don't you believe me? I've been walking. Don't you remember Rupinder?"

"Julie, I'm coming over and bringing a movie."

Julie put down the receiver and turned the volume up higher.

* * * *

"Shit! Goddamn it!" Adrienne must have told Meagan. She'd have been unpacking her CD's and cassettes, looking for some mood music to celebrate their first free night together. It was after the revelation; the fighting; the despair; the rage, and the move. They needed special music to go with the dinner, wine, and candles. What she'd actually forgotten was the boom box with the tape inside.

If Julie had made it, she would have called it a seduction tape. "To Adrienne" was printed on both sides in blue felt pen. Simplicity roars. "To Adrienne." Here. Here are all the things that I cannot say to you because I am afraid or inarticulate. Here is everything inchoate that I have named passion. Through these songs, please need me like I need you and fall hard in love with me.

The boom box had opened as slowly as a drawbridge. Julie held the tape for a long time before she played it. She looked at it and looked at it and looked at it, turned it over and looked at it some more. How could something so innocuous be so devastating? It was much easier to erase ideas. "I think my girlfriend has a lover" can be dissolved with enough denial, concentration, and distraction. Holding overwhelming evidence is a different matter. Julie held the physical proof of sickening betrayal. She held the formula from beginning to end, from the word 'go'. Julie was now privilege to Meagan's process. She had considered dubbing the tape and marketing it. *Now you too can find romance! Meagan Johnson shares her secrets. Decades of experience.*

We start with a few upbeat tunes to kick things off on a carefree, auspicious note, then a couple to fuel anticipation and expectation. Following these, a few brash and sexy celebrating new intimacy, and now we move into the moody, angry, loner-type tunes, just so you know how hard it is to live in this world with a brain like mine; and finally a not-so-sly segue into the final assault of pathetic ballads. *I Will Always Love You* (god, Meagan), *I Will Give You Everything.* Are you listening, Adrienne? Are you reading between the lines? Do you understand *me?*

After it had survived the hammer, Julie listened to the tape non-stop for three days. She wasn't sure what inside had halted her halfway to the utility drawer in the kitchen after she had played it and realized that it was not the first time she was hearing it. She was not sure what miraculously strong hand of restraint had intervened when she realized that Adrienne had had the audacity not only to smuggle the tape inside the house, but also to play the vile thing when Julie was at home!

Voice by voice, tone by tone, Julie had absorbed every note and dissected every lyric of the progressively desperate order of the songs. Only the first time was it shattering.

Julie knew that television, movies, and songs were the subsurface resources from which Meagan extracted her vocabulary, opinions, and virtually every form of physical expression (she could do the *Friends* cast flawlessly). "Books are useless," Julie recalled her saying from the dinner. So Julie concluded that the equivalents of all of Meagan's actions could be found in any television soap opera. Meagan would initiate nothing outside of these boundaries. Julie realized these parameters and identified them as a weakness. She figured she could always be one step ahead and, with that advantage, she could get Adrienne back.

Chapter 3 - Mystery Vegetables

Meagan stepped out of the pentagonal glass shower cubicle onto the mat and reached for a thick burgundy towel. It was the shower that had made her take the apartment. None of her friends had anything like it. They came over just to use it. It was a smart move by the owner, who bragged that because of it, the suite was never empty.

She faced the large bathroom mirror and patted her body dry. No rubbing, patting only. Pat, pat, pat. She took a black comb and slicked back her hair. She looked at herself down to just below her navel as far as the mirror went. She picked up a pair of tweezers and began plucking hairs from around her lips and chin. She winced in the mirror as she tried to grab a couple of elusive nose hairs. She slapped on Old Spice deodorant and a generous slather of Renegade cologne. She pulled a Q-Tip out of a plastic container and swabbed the inside of her ears. Don't push too hard. Remember the Ballpoint Pen Murders. She smiled contentedly at herself. "Today's the day," she said and flexed her arms into the mirror proudly.

* * * *

"Wait. I want to ask you one thing," said Sarah.

"What?" said Julie.

"Did you ever love me?"

Julie and Sarah exploded with laughter on the floor of Julie's apartment. Adrienne had used the key she still had and taken the couch. "I hope they're enjoying my couch," giggled Julie. "Moving right in together. Big mistake. Wait till the romance wears off. Big trouble."

* * * *

Meagan sat in the waiting room next to a dirty, small aquarium with murky water, a tipped-over miniature castle, and some scummy, self-flagellating plants until the doctor came out to get her. "Hello, Meagan. How are you today? Come on in."

Meagan followed Dr. Seitz into the examination room.

"So, another chemical peel, right? I usually like to wait a little longer between treatments, but you say there's been no irritation?"

"Nothing."

"Well then, you're familiar with the procedure by now, but do you have any questions before we begin?"

"No, I've been very satisfied . . . and I'm very attracted to you."

"Meagan, I'm flattered but . . . ."

"I've been feverish."

"Meagan, I don't mean to minimize your feelings or sound arrogant, but I get a lot of crushes. It comes with the territory of being an openly lesbian doctor serving our community."

"I get a lot of crushes, too. This isn't a *crush;* it's passion."

"Meagan, I find you attractive and intelligent, but I have a partner, and so do you. We've been together seven years."

"Seven-year itch. Can you look me in the eye and truly say that you're satisfied? Are you *denying* the current between us?"

"Meagan, you're making things awkward. I've made my position clear, and I reiterate that I'm flattered, but that's as far as it goes. I have to draw a line between the professional and the personal. Emotions get left at home."

"I won't come for treatments anymore . . . starting today."

"That's your decision, Meagan."

Meagan stood up and walked to the door. She put her hand on the doorknob, turned around and said, "I'm the best lesbian you'll ever have, Doctor."

* * * *

Julie was too tired to be livid for most of the day anymore. She was too tired to do anything but eat dinner on the floor propped against the wall on pillows. Like images hacked carelessly from an original painting, the apartment had become conspicuously bare. Photos were gone from the wall; books were gone from the bookcase, and clothes were gone from the closet. The same simple act of removing one's things to another place could either be blandly neutral or emotionally explosive; it's the difference between getting rid of something, or it being taken at the fractious end of a relationship.

"That's one of the worst movies I've ever seen," said Julie.

"I know," agreed Sarah.

"Who suggested you rent it, or did Meagan make it? Ha ha."

"Someone posted it on Divanet."

"What we'll endure for lesbian content, hey? Pathetic, though Charlene was beautiful."

"Yeah, she's my type."

"She's everybody's type, Sarah."

"Hey, Julie."

"Yeah."

"Do you think Uma Thurman would like me if she met me? Do you think she'd think I was cute and interesting, or do you think that she'd totally ignore me?"

"I think she'd like you."

"Really? You're just saying that."

"No, I'm not. I'm serious. I think you two would get along. Nothing's so great about Meagan, you know," moaned Julie. She rolled onto her side and pressed her head into a pillow. "I'm not the only one who thinks so, either."

"I know, Jules, but you do know that she volunteers to walk seniors' dogs?"

"No way."

"Way."

"Really?"

"Yes."

"She only works out her arms, you know. Lisa told me."

"Really?"

"Yesssssss, then she wears those sleeveless shirts. How vain can you get?"

"So that's why she's always wearing those. Don't let her drive you crazy, Jules. Consider the source. If you did that, then she'd never get to you again."

"Why does she always get a girlfriend, then, this source; a good girlfriend? Remember that story about the guy who isn't the best-looking, but gets the cheerleader because of his imagination? She's even low on that. She's a fraud desperately trying to construct the image of the artist. She assails the weak and then congratulates herself."

"Don't start, Julie," said Sarah quietly.

"Oh, I wish I were invisible. Then I'd drive her crazy. I wouldn't go in there and just hack her to death. No, I'd slowly torture her mind. I'd sail clothes right past her in the air. I'd put the milk right back in the fridge. And I want all my letters to Adrienne back, too. I bet you the writer/director doesn't write letters. I put effort into it, Sarah. You know how much."

And the notes! Julie thought. Notes on Adrienne's pillow and notes on the counter for when she came home telling her how much she was loved. Notes inside the microwave to make her smile, don't burn them up! Cold notes taped inside the fridge. Notes tucked into her lunch. Felt pens and markers and *good* paper.

Sarah put a pillow over her head and tried to block out Julie's voice. "Adrienne's not going to give them back to you, Jules."

"What did you say?"

"I SAID that Adrienne's not going to give them back to you."

Julie leaned over and ripped the pillow off Sarah's staticky head. "They're rightfully mine. I'm the author and I want them back."

"But you wrote them to her, so she is the rightful owner now."

"I wrote those letters to a *different* person. They were never intended for the person she is now, and they were non-transferable, so I want them back. I could get a lawyer. How much does a lawyer cost? I am not going to have my love letters there for her and Meagan to go over and laugh their heads off. Mocking me. Anybody could be reading them."

She had written what she thought were the answers for the two of them and sent them in dark-red envelopes, hot-pink envelopes, airmail envelopes, oversized envelopes, pristine invitation-white envelopes. The paper was thick; blue, green, pink, yellow, bought by the sheet. She used scratchy, fast-writing pens on paper from yellow-lined pads, not pieces torn raggedly from notebooks. Adrienne's address had been copied repeatedly on scrap paper to eliminate any initial fumbling: diagonal, in a neat line, in pyramid style, wherever it could be squeezed onto her doodling paper. Over and over her name was practiced so it wouldn't be slanted or sloppy. Adrienne Tessier. Miss Adrienne Tessier. Ms. Adrienne Tessier. Mr. Adrienne Tessier. Adrienne Tessier I. Julie Tessier. Julie and Adrienne Tessier. Mr. & Mrs. Adrienne Tessier. Julie Bell-Tessier. Adrienne Tessier-Bell. Julie and Adrienne Bell. The Bells. The Tessiers. She saw her face when she pulled it out of the mailbox. She was holding a mundane stack except for one gorgeous envelope with her beautifully scripted name on it.

"Oh god. I can barely stand to think about the paper trail that I've left in my life, Sarah; now multiplied to infinity by e-mail. Anyone could document my pathetic attempt at postal romance. It's humiliating. What an idiot I am! Have love letters ever gotten me anywhere? A big, fat NO! Why, why, why have I continued to put it down on paper all these years? That's it! I'm cured. Never again!"

"I understand what you're saying, Julie, but she's not going to return them, so you'll just have to face up to it."

"How can I get them back?"

"I don't know. Just forget it."

Julie sat up. "I have to break in there." She slapped her hand on her knee as if punctuating the sentence. "It's gotta be that. I have to break in. It's only on the second floor, so I can climb up onto the balcony. Maybe the door will be left unlocked; Adrienne's careless that way."

"Are you out of your mind? Just forget it."

"Well, how else can I get in there? Maybe I can bribe the cleaning lady."

"They have a cleaning lady? From Maid For You?"

"You're funny. I wouldn't accept them as clients if they were the last people on earth. I don't know, maybe they hired one of our competitors. That's something Meagan would do. It's their mistake if they did, though. Sloppy. Or maybe I could do the caretaker a sexual favor to get in."

"You're insane. Enough! Have you thought about this weekend, Julie? Are you still gonna come? I think it would be good for you. We always have a good time."

"I'll think about it."

* * * *

The phone rang and Julie picked it up. "Maid For You, Julie speaking. May I help you?"

"Hi, Jules."

"Oh, hey Colleen."

"So, have you decided yet? Are you coming?"

Julie had always enjoyed the weekends at Colleen's, but things had been strained between them since the break-up. Even though she knew that Colleen was trying to remain neutral, she had been bitter about Colleen inviting the snakes to a party while she was away. Philosophically, she could remain calm, but emotionally, she still boiled over.

"I don't know."

"They won't show up. Come on. It will do you good."

"Like it did all of you good to go to Goldfinger, Colleen? Just how was that anyway? You never did give me many details."

"Oh, Christ, Julie. I thought we were over that. What was I supposed to do, not go?"

"Go out with your true friends, not lying dogs. You might as well say it was right, then. It was right, Colleen? Fucking around for all those months; Meagan eating pizza in the same room for one reason only--to case us out. I am there having dinner with my girlfriend who loves me back at the time, but that is of *no* significance to dykes. Suddenly I am not a lover anymore; I'm a hindrance, an obstacle like one of those popping heads on a video game. Suggesting Chilean wine when she can't drink it because snakes have no lips. Those are the kind of people you want at your parties, Colleen?"

"Julie, please don't keep dragging me into the middle."

"I thought I was your friend."

"You are. I know you want me to hate them, Julie, but I can't. They didn't do anything to me."

"They devastated your friend and business partner. I'd say that's something."

"Julie, Maid For You is separate. Don't drag work into it."

"Oh sure, I know. Don't bring it here. Check your personal problems at the door, Julie. Leave your emotions at home; this is the office. Well, I can't help it, but I *cannot* divorce myself from my emotional life, Colleen. It's the essence of me. Everything that I care deeply about runs right through me twenty-four fucking hours a day, even when I'm dreaming people chase me and it's impossible for me to turn it on or off or leave it at the door like a coat! As one of the owners, I am allowed to be upset at the office!"

"All right, Jules. You decide, but we'd all like to see you."

* * * *

Lauren came into Julie's office and sat down in the beige armchair across from Julie's desk. She put her plastic bag of work clothes on the floor and nestled it between her feet. Julie smiled and motioned that she would be only a few seconds completing the call she was on. Lauren smiled weakly and turned her attention back to kneading the bag between her toes.

"Hi, Lauren," said Julie as she put down the phone. "Thanks for coming in."

"Sure."

"You probably know why I called you in here. We had another complaint yesterday. Apparently you left a gob of toothpaste in the sink and didn't empty one of the waste baskets."

"Sorry, Julie."

"I'm concerned. You're not usually sloppy. You've been with us for a long time now, and your record is--no pun intended--spotless."

"I'm sorry, Julie. I haven't been getting a lot of sleep lately. Things have been bad at home."

"I'm sorry to hear that, Lauren, but we have to leave our personal problems at the door. Will it help to talk about it? I'm here for you, you know."

"Thanks, Julie. I'm okay. It won't happen again. I promise."

"That's what you said last time, Lauren. We can't afford it again, and neither can you. If it happens again, I'll have to suspend you. I hate this part of my job, but I don't see any other choice."

Lauren levitated the plastic bag and lowered it down slowly. "I understand, Julie."

When she and Colleen had started their own cleaning company, Maid For You (They received continual flak from d.dee to change the company name. *Maid* is derogatory.), Julie never thought that she would be working more hours. She now had less free time, and the advantage of being the boss had never materialized, no putting in the office; no feet on the desk. Any sexual allure or advantage was nonexistent, and now sloppy work was forcing Julie and Colleen to abandon spot checks and check every job like they had done in the beginning. Work was wearing both of them down. If she had a choice, Julie would flee management and go back to cleaning.

Julie tried to concentrate on the schedule she was trying to make. Pieces of paper with employee requests for various days off were lying all over the desktop. No matter how diligently she tried to keep them all organized in one pile, they inevitably became separated and shabby, isolated from the original group, like scattered relatives in a Florida hurricane. Vacations, doctor appointments, weddings; considering the human element, she thought, it was a miracle anyone could keep a business running.

Schedule, Colleen's party, schedule, Colleen's party; Julie was engaged in a familiar debate with herself. Should she finish her work or should she go out socializing for pleasure? Actually, debate wasn't truly accurate. It had been a long time since she had had an authentic debate with herself; it was more like a justification ritual. *How late can a person be expected to work on a Friday night? This is a lot of overtime this week. Successful managers must know the recipe of equal parts work and play.* She had already made up her mind to go, but she had to run it past herself over and over until the struggle was prolonged enough so she could declare aloud, *Okay, I am going.*

Julie drove the monotonous highway out to the Schwartz Bay ferry terminal. Outside the last suburb, the land opened up onto narrow pastures of weak-green and parched-yellow grass. The relatively straight, flat line of the highway revealed the topography in clumps; clumps of trees, clumps of cows, and clumps of billboards. It was a disappointing scene coming upon the terminal, for usually when anticipating water the mind visualizes things like a sparkling sea; a secluded, tropical island, a soothing lakeside resort, or a spectacular waterfall. Here the water was drab, and vehicles were parked on the low, rocky sand where the beach should have been. Grave people readied fishing tackle beside open vans. The water was a dirty gray that took on a scheduled fierceness, churning the garbage and seagulls around the huge concrete pillars every time the massive ferries came into dock. The highway ended in a sprawling parking lot; a parking lot in the middle of the sea. No wait, only on the edge of the sea; a parking lot with a tower. Who's the king of the castle?

She pulled into her assigned lane and turned off the car to wait for the loading announcement. She looked around the crowded parking lot and tried to estimate how many cars were ahead of her. She squinted out to the vast, black, still water, but it was too dark to see anything approaching. That ramp did not look secure. Her mind wandered to the many times that she and Adrienne had sat in the ferry line-up together. It had felt so safe with Adrienne beside her, packed bags in the back. They'd sit up on the outside deck as the ferry sliced through the water. It didn't matter if the water was choppy or as still as night-time pavement on a deserted street; all that mattered was that they would be sleeping safely together in the same bed that night.

* * * *

And what were those factors that had combined in alchemical destiny to place Adrienne and Julie sleeping safely in the same bed? Psychologists and self-help experts might venture the explanation as the predictable success resulting from positive visualization about an ideal soul mate. Cynics, on the other hand, might attribute it to the predictable success of obsessively staking out a bar every weekend.

"You wanna come with me tonight, Sarah?"

In the weeks after she had first seen Adrienne in the casino, Julie had become a regular at Rumors. She knew that Adrienne would show up one day. It was the only bar in town. She had to show up.

Two months and sixteen days after Julie had seen her in the casino, on a Friday night, Adrienne Tessier walked, accompanied, through the door of Rumors. Julie was hanging around a pool table watching hapless Sarah lose.

"And so she just gave you the money for the Streisand tickets?" asked Sarah incredulously after she missed another shot. "Just like that?" Sarah usually blurted out some kind of chatter after shooting in the belief that it would distract people from her futility.

"Yup," replied Shelley. "Cashed in a mutual fund."

"So, with that poor girl's money you took your ex to see Barbara in Las Vegas?"

"That's right. Once in a lifetime chance, never happen again. You should have seen the beautiful, purple dress I wore."

"I can't believe that."

"Besotted, my dear Sarah, besotted. Only had to kiss her. It's good that was all it was, too. I never would have gotten rid of her had it been anything else," said Shelley with a laugh. Sarah did not join Shelley in the laughter and was unable to conceal her displeasure. Shelley noticed and added, "I didn't twist her arm, Sarah. It's a free country. If she wants to give away her money, that's her business."

"I don't know if I'd advertise that, Shelley."

"I'm not advertising anything." Shelley flipped her thick, long brown hair over her shoulder and picked up her bottle of beer. She pointed it at Sarah and said, "You asked me, and I'm telling you. It's not my fault that I can get anybody I want, and that I can make her do anything. Trust me. You would if you could. Cheers. Your shot."

"Sarah! Sarah!" Julie interrupted. "Sarah, she's here!"

Though she couldn't clearly see Adrienne's face, her form was enough to alter Julie's entire body chemistry. Instantly the dullness became so acute it could have ripped her wide open, and she didn't dare wonder how she could have existed second to second without her.

Her date paid their cover charges to the sullen young woman in leather pants at the door and then took hold of Adrienne's arm and escorted her into the bar. Adrienne wore a low, black, v-neck sweater and gray pants with a perfect stiff crease. *Oh my god, they are coming over here,* panicked Julie. *Oh my god, my hair. Last week's hair was way better. Why tonight?*

She hadn't had a chance to fix her hair. Adrienne's date walked up to the chalkboard and wrote, "Kirsten" on it. Adrienne and Kirsten put their drinks on the small, round table next to Julie and Sarah's table. Adrienne leaned against the stool next to Julie.

Julie bolted. "Drink, Sarah?"

She just needed a minute. When she returned, she gave Adrienne a big smile as she set the drinks down. She quickly looked to see if Kirsten was watching. Good. She was talking to someone. It's so transparent, she thought. Kirsten would know what she was doing. She would know. She would be able to read it. Dates could always tell. Keep your back to Kirsten whenever possible.

"Hi," said Julie.

"Hi."

"Are you playing?" asked Julie.

"No, I'm really terrible. Just watching."

"Me, too. I suck." As soon as the word *suck* had left her mouth, Julie regretted it. *Suck* wasn't cavalier. It wasn't suitable in an initial conversation with someone who had a perfect stiff crease in her pants. It was a blunt, harsh sound, even a little vulgar with the possible implications. What a stupid choice of words! Why did she have to go and say *suck* for? What if she hated that kind of talk? Oh great. What if she thought that she had meant that she sucked, too? Oh god. Why did she choose that word? She was so stupid sometimes. "My name's Julie," she said quickly.

"Hi, I'm Adrienne. You look familiar."

Maybe I look familiar because for seventy-seven days I have thought of little else but you and you felt it. Maybe it's because for seventy-seven days I have willed you to come here and find me. I have dreamt about you when I had no control and daydreamed about you when I could place my mind anywhere. Maybe that's why I look familiar. Instead Julie said, "I think I saw you at the casino once."

"That's it."

Meanwhile, Kirsten and Sarah had figured out that they had met before through d.dee. Kirsten was the Publisher, Editor-in-Chief, Layout and Design Coordinator, Sales and Marketing Manager (as well as regular contributor; in fact, the first time she wrote the entire issue) of *Sappho's Girls,* a lesbian newsletter that she hoped to turn into a magazine one day. d.dee had responded to Kirsten's pleas for contributions and submitted a short story and was still waiting to hear if it had been accepted or not. Kirsten told Sarah that since the call for submissions had gone out, she had been swamped by contributions, and the editorial decision regarding her girlfriend's story was pending.

Adrienne and Julie were able to converse mostly uninhibitedly that night because Kirsten, on finding out that Sarah wrote too, spent a great deal of time trying to convince her to submit a short story or some poetry, even a column. Kirsten could not then believe her good fortune when it was also discovered that pool hustler, Shelley, drew. Kirsten enthusiastically explained the new project that she planned to start after the newsletter had turned into a profitable magazine and she had gained all the necessary on-the-job-experience.

"A lesbian comic book! Kind of risqué. You illustrate, and I do the dialogue. We could make it great! I know we could get sponsors."

"What makes you think that I would want in any way to collaborate with you?" replied Shelley.

Kristin was only down a short time but rebounded when an entire new crop of undiscovered volunteers began pouring in for the Friday night. Thus it was easy for Adrienne and Julie to exchange phone numbers on a matchbook cover unnoticed and each slip the treasure into her pocket.

* * * *

Tense, Julie drove her car over the ramp and into the mouth of the ferry, parked and went upstairs for a coffee and a hot dog wrapped in aluminum foil. She took it outside and sat up on one of the outside bins. Her thoughts alternated between then and now, then and now, with her, without her, with her, without her. Now she was heading to Colleen's parents' cottage alone; then, she would have been going there with Adrienne. Why did this love have to turn into something so painful? She remembered when she couldn't wait to know more details about the girl. What kind of car did she drive? What kind of jobs had she had? Julie would get delirious rushes of happiness while piecing together the specific details that comprised the life of Adrienne Tessier. She looked at these kinds of details every day at work when cleaning someone's home. Shoes, what kind of shoes do they have? Knickknacks? Toiletries? There is no need to search for hidden journals that usually said the same thing anyway: "Got up at seven. Toast for breakfast. Worked hard all day. Tired. Why doesn't H. love me? I am so lonely I could jump off the bridge."

Even your garbage betrayed you. Looking for a mate? Blind dates fail again? Abscond with an object-of-your-affection's bag of trash, and then you'd know something. More revealing than a personal ad, is how Julie put it when she was trying to convince Sarah to accompany her on a stakeout of Adrienne's dumpster.

The Trash Detail had occurred in that frenetic period somewhere between their first words at the bar and the first date two months later. By Julie's constant badgering and sanitizing of the procedure, Sarah's initial repulsion was eventually worn down to a hesitant acquiescence.

"Look, you don't even have to look in the bag, though it's going to be really, really interesting. You're not too likely to get another chance like this in your lifetime, Sarah. Basically, you're just there as moral support and an extra pair of eyes. And if you do decide that you want to dive in, then you just slap on the latex gloves. It's fun wearing those gloves, like a crime scene investigator."

"I already have occasion to wear them, dearie."

"Oooooh, please don't get graphic, but I'm glad that you brought that up. What you and d.dee do is no less disgusting than what I am proposing. It's like being a scientist or a surgeon. Don't you ever want to try different things in your life? Think outside the box?"

"What if there are tampons in there, or pads?"

"Oh, big deal. Like you've never seen or touched any of those in your life."

"Not someone else's. That's revolting."

"Not d.dee's? Think of where your fingers have been all your life, Sarah, and it ain't pretty. It would be good. I could chart her period; it would help me decide when the best time to ask her out is."

The plan was beautifully executed on a Tuesday night. Wednesday was collection day in Adrienne's area, and Julie bet that sometime Tuesday evening Adrienne would walk out the back door to discard a bag of garbage. Nobody liked to trudge to the garbage bin looking ratty in the morning. At about nine-thirty the back door swung open and Adrienne appeared. Julie pulled down her baseball cap and punched Sarah on the shoulder jubilantly. "I knew it! The odds were in favor of nighttime. Look at her cute jean shorts." Julie peeked up into the rearview mirror and tried to ascertain what kind of bag she would be looking for. "Looks like just plain, white plastic, right?" She waited about two minutes after Adrienne had kicked the stopper out of the door and gone back inside. "Okay, cover me."

"Sure thing."

"I'm serious. I mean if she suddenly comes back out, then honk the horn or something. Distract her."

"Hurry up and go get it."

Julie tiptoed to the bin, peered into the side that was propped open, retrieved the bag and sprinted back to the Volvo. She jumped in the passenger side panting. "Drive!" She put Adrienne's garbage bag at her feet and nodded approvingly. "She ties a nice knot."

It was like coming home with a new stereo that she couldn't wait to get out of the box. Triumphantly, Julie spread out the contents of Adrienne's trash on her kitchen table that she had laid with newspapers. "You don't have to watch," she said to Sarah.

"I might as well now that I'm here."

"Seeeeeee, I told you it was interesting. Come on. Admit it."

"It does hold a certain fascination."

Looking like exhibits in a court trial, Julie tenderly and methodically laid out: two stringy, black banana peels, four small, plain, yogurt containers, a Kraft Dinner box, soggy brown pieces of lettuce, perhaps spinach, a fifty milliliter pink grapefruit juice container, orange peels, two apple cores, eight used coffee filters, an empty cream carton, an empty milk carton, tissues with lipstick, a clump of dark brown hair, four empty Winston Menthol cigarette packs, and one toilet paper roll.

"Good quality coffee. It still smells good," Julie told Sarah while holding up a used filter to the light with tweezers. She put the filter to her nose and sniffed again. "Blue Mountain. Maybe Kilimanjaro? Couldn't lose with a coffee date, could we?"

"Not only coffee, remember what I told you? This is important," said Sarah gravely. "It's better to do something like go to a movie first, or a play, something where you don't have to make uninterrupted conversation for an extended period of time. Dinners are high-risk, Jules. Successful, lingering dining is pretty tough to pull off the first time.

Movies are the ticket. Awkward conversation is minimized, and you get to sit side-by-side in the dark; that's the eventual goal anyway. It's twenty times better than sitting uncomfortably across from each other in a restaurant with people around you eavesdropping. It's a softer way to get used to her. People look decent with the lights down, so that worry is eliminated, too. And then, when it's all over, you have something to discuss over coffee. If it's not working, don't do coffee. With dinner, there is no escape. If it's bad, it's really bad, and you have to suffer the entire thing. Trust me; a movie's best."

Sarah declined a sniff.

"Good quality multi-ply tissues indicate an absence of stinginess. That's good to know right off-the-bat. Unsweetened juice, health-conscious, but smokes; that's always good for leverage, and I see compatibility staring right at me from that Kraft Dinner box."

* * * *

The car crawled slowly over the ferry ramp and merged into the lane that would eventually take her to Parksville. Every year for the last five years, the girls had held a weekend there while Colleen's parents attended a summer golf camp.

Why am I willingly going into the dragon's den? Julie wondered as she drove. Things are strained with Colleen, and d.dee will be running the show as usual. Her mind went back again. Julie and d.dee had detested each other on sight. That fateful night at Rumors, Julie called it. Sarah had gone missing and then reappeared with a tipsy d.dee clinging onto her arm. It was the instant jealousy and resentfulness that so often materializes between best friends and lovers, with nothing ever able to lessen it.

Julie held it in through a week of Sarah hurrying their phone calls, not being available for coffee, and talking exclusively about d.dee's world view. Nothing was safe from segue into d.dee. I like this blue shirt. Blue is d.dee's favourite colour. So it surfaced.

"What kind of name is that anyway, d.dee, no capitals, all small letters? It's supposed to be all one name, not two? You need two names in this world?"

"No, you don't," rebutted Sarah. "Madonna, Sting, Cher. It's more than a name. It's a statement. It shows that she's not buying into . . . ."

"She's hardly in that league. What's her real name?"

"That *is* her real name."

"No, it's not. No one named her small letters d.dee."

"Yes, it is her name. She got it legally changed."

"From what?"

"I'm not allowed to say."

"Why not? You can tell me."

"No, I can't."

"Yes, you can."

"Come on. I won't say anything."

"Yes, you will."

"No, I won't."

"Karen!"

"Karen what?"

"Kaufman. Don't you dare tell her I told you!"

"Now, what is wrong with the good Christian name of Karen?"

"I don't think it's Christian."

"Whatever. And by the way, *what* did Karen have on her head that night? Someone should tell Ms. Kaufman that corduroy caps have *never* been fashionable."

* * * *

Julie pulled into the gravel driveway and parked. When she entered the cottage, she was immediately dragged into joining the board game in progress.

"Okay, Newcomer," read Colleen from the box of cards, "How did Inspector Sullivan know that the lady in black was a fraud?"

"Don't know," said Julie. "Don't have a clue."

"Other team's open question for the same points."

"I know. I know!" yelped d.dee, "Because Cape Town is the legislative capital. *Pretoria* is the administrative capital."

"*Very* good, d.dee," complimented Sue. "Excellent!"

"You must have had this question before," said Julie.

"I did not. Besides, this is the first year that we've had this game here. I just know that answer. That's all."

"You must have read the cards through beforehand, then."

"I *did* not! I just know the answer."

"*How* would you know something like that?"

"Because I read."

"Yeah, the cards."

"Fuck you, Julie."

"I can't get any of these answers," said Julie. "Anyone for a walk?"

With beers in hand, Julie, Colleen, and Lisa headed down to the water. It shone black and polished. Colleen and Julie searched the damp shore for flat rocks to send skipping. One, two, three times, plunk. Colleen sent one over seven times. They drank their beers and listened to the water. "I could live out here all year round," said Julie. "It's so peaceful."

"Naw, you'd get bored soon and want to move back to the city," said Colleen. "There's not much to do. It's a good place to visit."

"Yeah, and you'd . . . ohmygod," said Lisa.

"What?" asked Julie.

"*Oh my god!* I think I left a candle burning at my place!" Panic replaced the serene look that had only seconds before been on Lisa's face. Her eyes darted pleadingly from Julie to Colleen and back, imploring them to provide reassurance that it wasn't so.

"Are you sure?" Colleen asked.

"No, not one hundred percent. I just can't remember blowing it out. Oh my god. I can't keep track of all these things. I just started saying 'stove is off' and never remember if I have said it or not. 'Candle is out' is too much, too ridiculous. What am I gonna do? It's too late to drive back!"

"Can't anyone in the building check for you? What about Louise? Can't you call her?" asked Colleen.

"No, she's gone away for the weekend, too."

"What about the landlady?"

"Gone. Everyone's gone. You know how old that building is, too."

"Haven't you ever fallen asleep with a candle going before?"

"Yes, but . . . ."

"Well, it just sputters out and dies, right? It doesn't set the place aflame. Has there ever been a fire before?"

"No, but this is that one time. That one time when the holder tips over and the tablecloth catches on fire and goes right up the curtains and the whole place is aflame!"

"Are you sure that you left it going?"

"Nooooooo."

"Okay, just think back . . . ."

* * * *

"She wrote, 'Well, you have to respect her need to breathe, and if you do that, then the extra weight doesn't necessarily have to be a problem,'" explained d.dee.

"Wow! What have we been missing?" asked Colleen. She and Julie had pacified Lisa with convincing arguments against an abode-engulfing fire and had returned to find the mood in the A-frame bolstered by a large alcohol intake.

"Oh, we're just debating some issues brought up at the last Womyn's Weekend regarding an advice column," explained d.dee.

"Someone lend me that magazine, will ya," said Julie. "Okay, here's one for y'all. So three dykes walk into a bar. One's Mexican, one's Polish and . . . ."

"I don't appreciate the sound of this, Julie," objected d.dee.

"What? Even before two complete sentences are out of my mouth, you are censoring me?"

"Ethnic humour is not . . . ."

"Okay, okay, forget it! Change it! Grasshopper walks into a bar, sits down and orders a whiskey sour. Grasshopper humor okay, d.dee?"

"Proceed."

"No, forget it, too. It's no fun anymore. You know what you are, d.dee? You're an enemy of comedy; a total crowd downer. It's frightening."

d.dee sighed and said, "There are a lot of people who don't consider that comedy, Julie. Anyway, I know that I will probably regret this, but are you interested in coming to the next weekend that I am helping organize?"

"You mean a Dyke Weekend?"

"You can call it that. Intent is to provide a precious lesbian space for . . ."

"Any cute girls giving workshops?"

"I'm offering a workshop, "Calculating Queer," where we will identify the demographics of mutual . . . ."

"I meant about safe sex or something."

d.dee gave another sigh before continuing. "Well, of course what you label 'sex' will be covered. How could we omit it? On the agenda is the dissection of the narrowly defined gender roles/essentialization of masculinity/ femininity/ imperial control of ethnic identity resulting in the historical marginalization of women that . . . ."

"I meant sex with me."

"You are so philistine, Julie. I don't know why I even *try* to take you seriously. You're obsessed with your common, savage needs and have not one inkling of the bigger picture."

"I don't want any of your inklings."

"Yeah, you don't want any of the world outside of Julie Bell's confining, underused brain. I knew that question earlier because I read; I absorb current events. I am concerned about the state of our civilization, about which you seem to have no care whatsoever. You are narrowly engrossed in your petty, primitive desires and have no--I hesitate to use the word, *humanitarian* concerns like I do."

"Oh, you're always talking about your big concerns. What concerns?"

"Well, for starters, my biggest concern right now is the over-consumption of resources in the Western Hemisphere. Do you ever take time to think about that?"

"Yeah, it keeps me awake every night."

"Exactly. Thank you for confirming my point. Nobody cares in this currency-based, rampantly materialistic culture. What happens when we run out?"

"Run out of what?"

"Of oil, for example."

"People are researching alternative energy supplies. You're not the only one to think about it. Are you designing solar panels or windmills? Why are you always trying to scare people with that and things like population numbers?"

"Not to mention the destruction of the rain forest," d.dee continued, "killing all those species that could cure cancer."

"Or cause it. There are species that haven't even been identified yet, according to what I've read."

"They write about that in *People?* You have to do more than just read, you know, action is required."

"Tell me, Action Queen, what do you do?"

"I try to buy only recycled goods . . . ."

"Which produces more pollution."

"You consume blindly, Julie, never giving a thought to what you are buying."

"You buy recycled because you never have any money."

"I buy recycled and environmentally-friendly, which is usually more expensive, for your information."

"You can afford that only because you subsist on cheap, mystery vegetables."

"What?"

"Nothing."

"I eat low on the food chain. It's only my little part, but I like to think it makes some small difference. It's something. Again, I don't see you doing anything, Julie."

"Low on the food chain? That ought to earn you a Nobel Prize someday."

As soon as she said this, Julie knew that d.dee's patience had come to an end. Her thin, dry face looked at Julie's and delivered what had been well-rehearsed. "I knew that it would be a waste of time trying to talk you into helping. Sorry, Julie, my mistake. No wonder Adrienne dumped you."

Julie's top lip pressed down onto the bottom one--such a slight gesture for such a great pain. "Well, at least I don't pretend to be something that I'm not. All of me is out there basically uncovered now," she shot back. "You should hear yourself, d.dee. You have no idea how ridiculous you sound, which is probably good because it would stun you like Charlie Brown watching home movies of himself. And your secret language, secret mumbo jumbo code. I had a secret mumbo jumbo code, too, when I was eight in our fort under the stairs. You want to be called brilliant. Lurking around the bookstores trying to look sexily intellectual and then grabbing the first thing when a cute girl comes by. Oh yes, yes, *The Rise of Popular Feminism in Peru.* It's not going to happen that way, d.dee. You should try Meagan's way. At least she gets results."

Chapter 4 - Noah's Vessel

Sure, dump me after I finally come out to my parents. I tried to present a stable, loving, alternative relationship; I tried to show them that for the first time in years their daughter was happy, and look what happened--good timing, Adrienne. This was the last thing I wanted to involve them in. I could do standup with this life, thought Julie. Where's Adrienne? How's Adrienne? Is anything the matter, dear? Oh, and my "put on your dyke uniform and march down Main Street, and if you ever need someone with the right kind of plumbing for one of your girlfriends, give me a call" brother is going to love this. Asshole.

It had been about a year since Julie had had her parents for *the* dinner. "Wonder what she wants?" her mother had probably asked her father after Julie had called to invite them. "Money? She's pregnant? How could that be when I never see a boy? She never invites us to her place, and she's cooking, too? It must be huge."

"It's imperative for me to be honest," Julie had told Sarah. "Don't hide anything. Be open. Be yourself. And most important, remember your self-respect. They may disown you, but you can hold your head up high. The same goes for when you tell your friends, too. These years of *Oprah* haven't gone unheeded, you know."

"They already know," Sarah had said.

"No, they don't."

"Yes, they do. They must have figured it out by now. Your mother watches *Oprah* too, you know."

"No, you don't understand them. They're totally old-fashioned. This would never cross their minds."

"It must have."

"No, I tell you, they are clueless that way. At least my father is. It's my mother I'm really worried about, and that's why I don't want Adrienne there, just in case Mom flips out."

"Not possible."

"Extremely possible. You don't know my parents."

At least with a coming-out dinner Julie didn't have to spend the day taking down lingerie posters and telltale party photographs or purging the house of incriminating literature. "We're worse than Roman Catholic school board trustees," Adrienne had observed. There was no need this time to duplicate the charade of making the spare room into Adrienne's bedroom, like on past occasions. "Looks like it's out of *Little Women* or something. That's a nice touch with the afghan in there, though. It will make your mother very pleased, Julie. It suits that room. I'm glad you took it off our bed anyway. You know how uncomfortable it makes me during sex."

What did one make for a coming-out dinner anyway, Chicken Surprise? No, something that pleased everyone was required, something with a cream sauce. That was it. Something that Mother would love, but wouldn't make herself because of the calories or because she had to buy butter.

In what she believed to be her most practical and rewarding New Year's resolution ever, Julie had vowed never to buy margarine or butter substitutes again. For once, she didn't abandon her bursting resolve, which usually was the result after only a few sober hours. For once, she didn't let her sincere, drunken promises evaporate into a puddle of jellyfish guilt. This seemingly mundane decision unexpectedly brought Julie a surging freedom. She diagnosed it as the dismantling of the small patterns that allowed her, and trained her, to take on the bigger ones.

"It may seem like a small thing to other people, Adrienne, but it's how you turn your life around, baby. I never wanted to buy that other crap. It was the price, only the price. I am tired of being dictated to by price! I'd stand in the grocery store and stare at the butter while one after another, people snatched the margarine out of the cooler. Then I'd pick up the margarine, too, and put it in my cart. Don't you see? I always felt cheap and dissatisfied after. I longed for the butter. How many other things have I longed for in my life? You pay if you repress these longings, you know, and I've paid, believe me."

"God, Julie, it's just a butter preference. Do you always have to be so dramatic?"

"NO! That's just it! That's the point. It's not just a butter preference; it's a big thing! It's the perfect example, Adrienne. I'm tired of longing. I love buying butter now. With pride I put it in my cart, snubbing all frugality. That one small decision can apply in all the bigger ways. You cook with butter. It matters. Can you imagine a dignified French chef in his whites explaining how to melt margarine? So, I'm writing it all up and someone is going to publish it. Maybe a 'letter to the editor'."

The buzzer sounded and interrupted Julie's daydream.

* * * *

"Hi, we're here."

"Hi, come on up."

Approximately forty-five seconds left in our previous relationship, thought Julie as she timed her parents on the second hand of her watch. Forty-five seconds only. She heard them coming down the hall and went and opened the door.

"Hi, Mom, Dad." She kissed them as they came in. Oh, how different it will be when you leave here tonight, she thought. You walked in the door as one thing, you got some information and then you walked out as something else. You came in as Mr. and Mrs. Bell, parents of *normal* daughter Julie, and you left as the parents of a deviant. Yes, as a matter of fact, I do have something for you to take home tonight. Would you like me to wrap it up in a doggie bag?

"This is for the hostess," said Mr. Bell.

"Oh, Dad, you shouldn't have," said Julie as she mechanically took the paper bag.

"It's Chilean," he said.

"Oh, great."

"It smells delightful in here," said her mother as she headed for the kitchen.

"Rosalie, we are the guests here and the first thing the guests do not do is go snooping around the kitchen. Come on. The living room is this way."

"It's okay, Dad. It's not Chicken Surprise. It's chicken breasts in a cognac cream sauce."

"Sounds suuuuuuper," said her dad.

"Even the name sounds better than anything I've ever made," said her mother. "Which mother did you learn that from? Can I peek?"

Julie watched her mother lift the skillet lid. "Let's save the wine for dinner," she said. "Can I offer you two a drink of something else? I have beer and some open white wine, and I think some Peach Schnapps left over from last weekend."

"I'll take a beer," said her father.

"Oh, is that Schnapps in that pretty bottle, Jim?" asked her mother. "Just a capful, even a capful makes me a little tipsy. By the way, Julie, I saw Mrs. Bennett and Barbara at the mall last week. Barbara has put on a lot of weight. Too bad, she's such a pretty girl. Goodness, it seems like just yesterday that the two of you were having one of your sleepovers and giggling all night. Couldn't tear the two of you apart."

That's right, encourage the small talk and then hit 'em with it during dinner, exactly as she had planned.

Halfway through her culinary coup, Julie felt that it was time to be open and honest. "Mom, Dad," her voice quivered, "Did you ever wonder why I wasn't married?" While she waited for the answer, she scraped the remaining food on her plate into little piles.

"No," said her father. He smiled at his daughter and took a satisfying bite of chicken breast sopped in cream sauce. Julie and her father both had thick, brown hair and wide, brown eyes that seemed never to blink. She knew that she should have kept her big mouth shut. Fucking Sarah. *She knew it.* Rosalie laid down her fork precisely and picked up her wine glass. She sat very straight. Julie watched her mother's tense face; her baseboard brown hair was pulled back, highlighting the intermittent gray semicircle of her face. Don't stop now. It would be worse. Don't stop now.

"Ummmm, well, the thing is that I've, I've, ummm . . . I've had boyfriends and girlfriends, and I am probably not going to get married. And right now I'm dating Adrienne. We're living together here as a couple. And that's about it."

The dazzling monologue that she had rehearsed wouldn't come out of her mouth, particularly the word *lesbian*. It sounded so dirty, especially in front of her mother. It reminded her of all the *True Confessions* magazines that she had read in elementary school, the ones that had first informed her about being a lezzie. She didn't want what she told her parents to sound creepy like they did. "We were all alone in the high school library when Grace put her hand on my elbow. It was then I *knew* that Grace was *a lesbian!*"

"Is there any more wine, please?" asked her mother. She bowed her head over her plate.

"Well, that's okay, dear," said her father as he looked at his wife for support and found that he wasn't going to get it. It was a familiar tilt of her head, the abandonment tilt. When he saw the uncomfortable, ashamed, angry head, he knew that he was on his own. "I don't really understand these things, honey. I'm kind of old-fashioned, but I know that's the way things are these days, and we love you regardless." He went back to his plate and sopped up all remaining sauce with the rice.

"Thank you, Dad."

Her mother didn't move.

"I told you," she said to her husband and then turned to Julie, "Your Aunt Frances is going to be so upset. I just don't know how I'm going to tell her."

"This is *not* about Aunt Frances," replied Julie calmly. She refilled her mother's wine glass and then her own.

"She's so prominent in the Church."

"You know how I feel about the Church."

"That's the problem. You've turned your back on religion, and these are the abominations that happen when you turn your back on God!"

"It's not that simple, Mother. I've turned my back on an institution whose leaders are continually accused of all kinds of molestation, primarily homosexual. How can you continue to defend it?"

"Don't blaspheme in my presence, and if you're referring to that movie about the priests again, that piece of trash . . . ."

"What are you going to do, Mom? You got Disney stock to sell?"

"It's all lies!"

"NO, they're not lies! Who has been perpetuating the lies with dogma that explains nothing? Save our children. Save our children from homosexual teachers, and now you're finally finding out that you've been targeting the wrong people all this time. Oops, you made a mistake. It's not gay teachers you have to protect your children from; it's priests, and teenagers going on shooting sprees. For once, face the real issues and stop thinking only about yourself and the neighbors. Think about me for once!"

"I've always thought about you! I've taken care of you since you were a baby. I just don't know how to explain this. I saw some of them on *Regis and Kathie Lee* and, quite frankly, I couldn't watch it. I don't understand it. What do girls do anyway? It's not normal!"

"Take a look at some of Dad's pornography stash in the basement sometime and you'll see what's not normal. Have you seen what's out there? Do you have any idea how sick some of it is?"

"Calm down, you two, calm down." Jim Bell had had considerable experience containing arguments between his two girls. "Don't be so angry with your mother, honey, and thanks for selling me out. It's so new to her, this kind of thing. She—we . . . just need some time to think about it all. We support you, honey, whatever you do. We love you, Julie. Rosalie . . . ." It wasn't a command; it was more like a firm urging, a calm plea for understanding and compassion, for his wife to give a little, if not for their daughter at this moment, then for her partner of over thirty years.

"We do love you, Julie," sobbed her mother.

The Apple Surprise remained untouched in the kitchen. Adrienne threw it away two days later.

* * * *

Sarah walked into Lavender's and slumped glumly down into the chair across from Julie. "d.dee and I are trying a trial separation," she announced.

Julie didn't look up from her magazine. "Again?"

"Thanks for being supportive. I'll remember that the next time you start whining about Adrienne. That last time didn't count. It was only a few days; this is the real thing."

"I didn't know that you two were still having problems, aside from the obvious ones, I mean. And just for the record, it was thirty-eight hours."

Sarah picked up the plastic menu stand and passed it from hand to hand. "I always listen to you."

"I know. I'm sorry, Sarah. I'm listening. Wow, what a pair we make. What's going on now?"

"Well, for starters, we spend waaaaaaaaay too much time together. We're too dependent on each other. We need some space. We've got to cultivate our own friendships and interests again, go on separate holidays, that kind of thing. I have inexcusably neglected my friends since d.dee and I started dating. I apologize for that. My personal ambitions have disappeared as well."

"You two don't go on holidays together now. You're always too broke. You went to Mexico with your family."

Sarah slammed the menu stand down, pushed her chair away from the table and angrily stood up. "I'm gonna go find someone else to talk to, someone who will . . . ."

Julie stood up quickly and grabbed Sarah's hand. "No, wait. Sorry, Sarah. Please sit down. You're right; I am selfish. Please sit down. I'm listening." She gently pressed her friend's shoulder to persuade her back into her seat. "I think that's a good idea. You're right; you spend way too much time together. So when did you decide this?"

"About thirty-six minutes ago," she moaned as she looked at her watch. She sat back down. "Of course, we won't avoid each other if we see each other and stuff, but we're not going to phone, and I'm not going to stay over at her place for about a month. We'll see what happens from there."

"Oh, a bachelorette! What about seeing other people during this period? That might be a good idea, you know. Take your own advice."

"We've decided that it's okay."

"Really? d.dee agreed to that, really? I can't believe it."

"She had to agree to it. This whole thing was her idea."

Julie sat up straight in her chair and pulled it closer to the table. "Do you think that she has an ulterior motive this time?"

Sarah sighed and her shoulders sagged. "You mean is she interested in someone else?"

"Yeah."

"No. In a way, I wish that were it. I think she wouldn't mind trying some dating, but it wouldn't go much past that. She's seriously not interested in anyone but me, though she is always trying to create that impression. You know what this really is all about, Jules? She wants me to miss her. She has orchestrated this entire thing just to get me to pine for her."

"That sounds like something I would do. Is it working?"

"It's been working for forty minutes, though I really think that these emotions are best left to materialize naturally. Don't you agree?"

"Oh, I agree. These little tests tend to backfire. Ask an expert. Remember Theresa? Remember when I told her that we would 'never see each other again'? I didn't mean it literally. She was supposed to crawl back and beg and say, 'No, no, not that, Julie, anything but that. I can't survive without you. Have mercy, please. Not that.' Instead she agreed. 'Like you said, we will never see each other again.' Instead of giving her the heartbreak of a lifetime, I gave her the avenue of escape. Paved it right to her doorstep. Oh Sarah, don't look now, but . . . ."

Sarah started to turn in her chair.

"I *said*," Julie hissed, "don't look now." She continued in a low, halting tone, trying to move her mouth inconspicuously. "I think that girl over there in the red is staring over here."

"Okay," whispered Sarah conspiratorially, "I'll do the magazine thing. Hold on." She eased her chair away from the table and got up. She meandered, what she thought was nonchalantly, over to the coffee table, stooped down and picked up a magazine. On the way there, she took two neck-wrenching, sideways glances at a girl in a red cotton jacket and jeans. On the way back, she did the same thing, only this time while turning a few pages of *Yachting* magazine.

"So, what do you think?" Julie asked when Sarah sat down again.

"Nope."

"What do you mean 'nope'? I caught her staring over here a couple of times."

"There's a purse on the chair. You know that's almost instant disqualification."

"And you know that I have never fully agreed with that classification."

"Only because it clashes with your wishful thinking. It's valid, Julie, whether you want to accept it or not. We don't carry purses. Face it. Some try, but it rarely looks natural. Even Adrienne only carried one sometimes, and she barely pulled it off. Why do you think OB tampons continue to be number one among lesbians? Because they fit in our pockets and knapsacks, that's why."

"She could be an exception. Anything's possible."

"Yes, you're right. You dated the exception, but as you like to say, the odds; I am going with the odds, Julie, and the odds say that she's not."

"All right," said Julie grumpily. "And do me a favor, next time, pick up a more convincing magazine. I still say that she was looking over here. Now, where were we? Oh, yeah. Are you all right with all this d.dee stuff?"

"Yeah, I'm fine. I would just like things to run smoothly for once, that's all. No histrionics."

"I hear you. Okay, well, how about Saturday night, then? Single, crazy and available just like the old days? By the way, did you think over what I asked you?"

"I'm not helping you with that, Jules."

"Come on, why not? It would be the perfect time now that you don't have to be at d.dee's every night."

"Look, I'm the one who found out where they're staying. The rest is yours. Especially after the garbage detail, I don't think that you can ask me these things anymore. I've done my part. I have done more than my part, Julie."

"It would be nice to have some company," said Julie. Her head tilted involuntarily to the left, and her lips pursed together in the tight half-smile that appeared whenever she was asking someone for a favor.

"Forget it! I am not spying on them with you. How old are you anyway? I thought you were thirty-two. I've too many other things to think about right now. I don't know why you want to do that anyway. It's not healthy, Julie. You're just gonna sit outside the B&B in your car all night?"

"Not *my* car. I've gotta get another car. Whose car can I get? They'd recognize mine . . . and yours."

"You continue to torture yourself over and over and over. They're going to be in there making love, Julie. Having sex, Julie. Why do you want to put yourself in that situation? How can you, anyway? You've got to move on."

"I just want to see her, and this is her birthday weekend. I bet she's been getting attention all week. Look at me, how wonderful I am, Adrienne. I remembered your birthday, now will you fuck me? I made this tape just for you, Adrienne. Every song means something. Now will you fuck me? That's what they remember it for. Not for her, but for themselves. Always strings."

"What about your own strings then, Julie?"

"I have to see her. I haven't seen her yet. I just want to look at her. A ghost can't do this to me, Sarah. At least then I know where she is, what she is going to do. I can't stand not knowing. If she's there, at least she hasn't left the city. She hasn't gone to Paris or New York. At least I know she's just in there with Meagan, and I know what they're doing and saying because Meagan is so predictable."

"What are you going to do when they go on a holiday someday to Mexico or Hawaii? Follow them?"

"Don't say that."

The Daffodil Bed and Breakfast – 'Catering to the Gay Community'- was run by longtime couple Jean and Edith who had been together almost thirty years. The Daffodil was famous for its quaint, romantic rooms (there were only six, so you had better book well in advance) and the healthy, delicious food. Jean and Edith themselves were also regarded as one of the alluring features of the establishment. Younger couples sought advice from them on the secrets of maintaining a long, successful relationship. It was not unusual to find one or both of the women in the dining room after dinner speaking in reminiscent tones over coffee, surrounded by eager listeners.

Relationships in all stages of success or disrepair had passed through the Daffodil, and even if it was only a temporary lifting of terminal symptoms, everyone left happier than when they went in. In the Lower Mainland community, "We're going to the Daffodil this weekend," was synonymous with happiness, love, sex and romance; in other words, the salad days.

Julie slouched in Sarah's cousin's car halfway up the eleventh block of Shakespeare Street. She had arrived two hours ago with a take-out latte, a newspaper, a copy each of *Girlfriends, People,* and *Newsweek* magazines and a crossword puzzle book. The crossword puzzle book was useless to her: "Noah's vessel" "Zsa Zsa's sister." She couldn't concentrate on that. The newspaper and magazines soon proved useless, too; flip, flip, flip. Wearing sunglasses didn't make it any easier to read, either. Only stirring the latte was able to occupy her.

The thin elms were little protection from the persistent sun. Even into early evening, the upholstery in the Honda was as hot as an electric blanket that had been left on all night. Julie had concluded that in a matter of pure logistics, their most probable approach to the Daffodil would be from the east. They wouldn't come some obscure route, now would they? Julie parked the inconspicuous Civic on the left-hand side facing south. As she had estimated, she had approximately only twenty-five seconds to watch them as they crossed the Shakespeare and James intersection and walked to the latticed gate. They arrived, consistent with all calculations, just before six. They wore dyke sunglasses and carried dry cleaning against their overnight bags. Julie hadn't been expecting any dry cleaning, and its celebratory nature particularly upset her. There was a pompous way that Meagan held the dry cleaning, like an arrogant, young businessman picking up a tux for his first formal dinner. She held the hanger stiffly in front of her like a shield with one hand and maneuvered Adrienne down the sidewalk with the other.

They would be celebrating Adrienne's release from Julie, her escape and flight to Meagan. Adrienne now packed her bag for that witch. Julie knew what was in that bag. Effortlessly she could mentally unpack the cream, shampoo, toothpaste, make-up, lingerie, and if she concentrated long enough, she could smell it there in the car, feel it there in the car. She looked at Adrienne's soft, reddish-blonde hair that curled against her neck about two inches below her ears. Adrienne walked with her head lowered, while Meagan held hers high. "Her head's never that high when she walks alone," said Julie as she threw the crossword puzzle book at the windshield. No, Meagan usually walked with her head down and a miserable, pre-emptive sneer on her face, hoping to affect the pose of a disinterested, sullen, androgynous model.

Meagan moved her hand from Adrienne's shoulder to her elbow and guided her towards the gate. It struck Julie now that she had seen the same thing before, but where? Was it when she had first seen Adrienne in the Towers Casino? Adrienne had held her chin in one hand and with the other pulled a cigarette in a distracted way to her small mouth. Her jade-green eyes never left the cards as the dealer rhythmically placed them from one square to the other. Like most amateur gamblers who were intimidated by the pace and rules, Julie had stood awkwardly fascinated behind the table. Sarah had kept nudging her, first to notice Adrienne, and then to sit down and join the game. Rather than watching Adrienne, Julie had watched the girl sitting to Adrienne's left on the second square of the blackjack table. She had bristly, short, black hair and wore a jean jacket and calf-high, black, shit-kicking boots. Adrienne was too advanced a blackjack player to need instruction or advice, so her date needed to remedy this lack of an avenue to parade that they were together. Like a child grabbing candy from a sibling, the woman repeatedly snatched chips from Adrienne's pile to play with, though she had a big pile of her own. It was the taunting and teasing of elementary school crushes; the adult version now permitted sexual innuendo. Had her date been a man and they'd been playing at separate tables, he would have run across the room on a shuffle break just to give her a kiss. No, not the casino. It wasn't there that she saw that movement from shoulder to elbow. It was in Rumours when she came in with Kirsten. Everything was blurring together now, and it was too exhausting and painful to differentiate.

Of course, Meagan would keep her hands all over her! Tears came quiet and softly hot down Julie's cheeks. She held the steering wheel and let them fall, not even trying to wipe them away. If it had been raining she could have gone outside for a walk and no one would have noticed. "How did I ever think I could keep a trophy wife?" she whispered.

Chapter 5 - The "F" Section

It had been a satisfying weekend at the Daffodil, thought Meagan as she stood in front of her full-length mirror. Sex had been steamy; Adrienne had fallen more in love with the gorgeous face she was now looking at. The mirror was a two-sided broad oval that hung on a mahogany frame in the corner of her bedroom. It was the kind of mirror that made you think that maybe, just maybe, when you flipped to the other side you would get something unexpected, something that wasn't there before. Like a funhouse effect, producing magnified or distorted dwarf and giant versions of yourself, or an ivy-covered secret entrance beckoning you; maybe a hideous, trapped, green ghoulish face. It might not be the same on both sides, so flip quickly!

But Meagan wasn't looking for a mirror built for illusions. She was looking for a mirror built for a couple. (Or was that the biggest illusion?) Had this mirror been designed by someone used to being the taller of a twosome, someone weary of always grooming behind the shorter partner and tired of intermittent glimpses of only the head and shoulders? Now two people could get dressed in comfort at the same time! Surely this would maintain the domestic harmony of couples since it was always the little irritations that spread into the big rashes. That's why it was perfect for Meagan, not because "harmonious" could ever have been used to describe any of her relationships, but just because Meagan was usually a couple. She didn't like to be alone. She couldn't measure herself when she was alone.

"This is perfect for me," she had said to her cousin Brenda, when she had first seen it. "It's an antique for sure." The state of being in a relationship was the only acceptable state to Meagan. Who would desire otherwise? She defined herself by her relationships. Meagan and: Meagan and Lisa; Meagan and Rupi; Meagan and Janice; Meagan and Fatima; Meagan and Kelli; Meagan and Iris; Meagan and Kylie; Meagan and Eleanor; and currently, Meagan and Adrienne.

Meagan stopped combing her hair and pulled her white, sleeveless tee shirt tight over her tummy. "You're gorgeous," she purred. She flexed her arms and turned for a side view. She smoothed her navy boxers admiringly down over the top of her legs. "I'll give you what you want, baby."

She went out to the living room, cranked the CD player, and then ran back into the bedroom to pose in front of the mirror again. She held the comb up to her mouth and began to sing to her reflection. "I'm a mess without my little China girl, Wake up in the morning where's my little China girl . . . I feel a-tragic like I'm Marlon Brando when I look at my little China girl." She threw her head back and, clenching the comb tightly, ran her hands downward over her breasts and slid her fingers together just below her navel.

"My little China girl, you shouldn't mess with me, I'll ruin everything you are. I'll give you television. I'll give you eyes of blue. I'll give you men who want to run the world . . . ."

She brought her hands back up to her mouth with the comb still between them. She put the index finger on her right hand to her lips, jutted out her neck, half-closed her eyes and leaned close into the mirror. "And when I get excited, my little China girl says, 'Oh baby just you shut your mouth,' she says, 'Sh-shshh. Sshhh.'"

David Bowie was in two places; tacked up above the bed where he was not in good shape, torn at the corners from all the times that he had been taken down and then stuck back up. If you looked carefully, you could find on the right side of his nose (your right, his left) a tear that had been glued together. It had to be fixed after Iris, enraged, had jumped up and tried to rip him from the wall. Though Meagan had tried to paste it together as perfectly as a jigsaw puzzle and line up any bold lines or continue a seamless blue on blue sky, it was still a little off, with the two sides of his injured nose now meeting fractionally crooked. David was also in the front room in a framed black and white picture, a present from Kylie, which she had believed at the time would make Meagan love her forever. Having David Bowie as one of her idols was more to Meagan than buying his music and hanging his picture in her home. Everyone did that, and she was not everyone. Meagan knew that their relationship was special. He was the one who reinforced in her that she was not an average person.

"Hot and androgynous, Brenda, that's the key," she often told her cousin. "I feel more. I experience more. I know more. I love more. I'm like David Bowie, his female counterpart. I could marry a model, too. You know, sometimes his music just makes me weep. 'Heroes, we can be heroes,' Brenda, and you know that Meagan Johnson does not cry."

With her hands now tightly on her ass, she did some Michael Jackson pelvis thrusts and then lowered herself to a crouch to catch her breath. "Do I have time?" She stood up, dragged the mirror to the end of the bed and then went over to the dresser. Rummaging to the back of the bottom drawer, she pulled out a black plastic bag. Out of the bag she took a seven-inch indigo-blue silicon dildo and tube of K-Y Jelly. She took everything to the bed and lay down on her back: one pillow for her head, one pillow under her lower back. She squeezed a blob of transparent jelly onto the dildo and then set the tube aside. She watched her reflection as she smoothed the jelly up and down and over the ridges of the dildo. With her knees spread wide, she began rubbing the cool tip very softly over her clitoris. With her middle and index fingers she parted herself and rubbed up and down and then in circles, pressing deeper each time. "Oh, baby. Oh, baby. Tell me to fuck you. Come on." She rubbed faster and harder.

"Oh, come on, baby." She teased herself and then begged herself to plunge. "Ooooh," she moaned as she pumped herself. "I love you so much. You like me fucking you, don't you? Is that what you want?" She jammed it in harder and harder. "You only want me to do it to you. I'm going to do it to you. I'm going to make you feel this. I'm going to fuck you so good. You're so pretty. I love you so much." Afterward she lay with the sticky, warm seven inches between her legs, drifting into sleep until an instinct jolted her. "Jeezus, Brenda is going to be here any second!"

Brenda had a key.

"Gotta get dressed."

* * * *

They sat at the Ikea table in the kitchen. "It has to say *professional* in it. It has to be very specific," said Brenda as she looked up from the notepad that she was writing on. "Are you even listening to me? Come on. This is important. You promised to help."

"I'm listening. I'm listening. But wait til you hear the dream I had last night. God, I woke up pumped up! It was so vivid. That's why I know it is going to come true someday, Brenda. In some form, it's going to come true. Then I am outta this town."

"*We're* outta this town. You promised."

"That's what I meant. Don't worry. I am a woman of my word, Brenda. Meagan Johnson keeps her promises. You know that. Okay, so here's the dream. I'm taking an English composition class, if you can believe it, and the first day I walk in and you should see the teacher! I think, hey, she looks like Catherine Deneuve, and I get closer, and it *is* Catherine Deneuve! She's standing in front of the board, effortlessly elegant, just beautiful. She can't take her eyes off of me as I find a seat. It's painful how none of the other women can compare. Week by week the intensity builds. The glances become smoldering looks. The electric current between us becomes almost unbearable. I don't know how we control it. Her touches border on caresses. She reads to us in English with her wild, sexy, French accent. She's feverishly beautiful in her love of creativity. She glides the aisles with her arms folded protectively over one of her precious books. By my desk she lingers. And then I write *the poem*. The poem that makes her say, 'Oh, Meagan, in all my years of teaching that was the best poem that I have ever read. You are truly the most gifted student that I have ever encountered. I'd like you to stay after class.'"

"Oh god," said Brenda.

"What? I'm meant for something like that. You'll see."

Brenda had a persistent, disturbing way of making you feel like how you feel at the end of a fantastic movie that you never wanted to end. You wanted to sit there and continue to bask in the magnificent manipulation of your senses, but the lights came on you were forced out of the theatre and into the cold street. She always made you feel just expelled from the cocoon, instantaneously and brutally stripped of your dark, warm dreaming place.

"Okay, and meanwhile I'm meant for only something like this. *Professional.* It has to have *professional* in it, doesn't it?"

"Yeah, definitely. You want someone in the same class, someone with the same values, someone you can relate to. If you don't put it in, then you'll just get anyone calling. And there are lots of weirdos out there, Bren, believe me. They may look normal on the surface, so you don't realize it until it's too late and then you're living together, and it's a big hassle to get rid of them. You remember Lisa's ex-roommate, that crazy Elise? The one who stole money and CDs from her and didn't pay her share of the utilities? Ran up huge long distance bills on Lisa's phone, ate all of her food, and on top of that, practically every week she'd lock herself in the bathroom and threaten to commit suicide? Remember?"

"Yes, I remember. And it's not exactly what I want to hear right now, Meagan." Brenda grimaced, unscrewed the cap on her Evian water, took a drink and then screwed it back on. "Okay, how does this sound so far? 'You are female. You are progressive. You are respectful. You are a professional. You love women. You are willing to share and respect space with a sensitive, tolerant Aquarius goddess. You preferably work days or all weekends . . . .'"

"Don't use 'respect' twice, and do you have to put 'Aquarius' in? Then it sounds like a personal ad, not a roommate ad."

"Well, I think it's important, and it will increase the chance of finding someone compatible. They'll know it's for a roommate. They can read."

"Okay, if you insist. It's your ad. I just can't emphasize enough to make sure that there's no sexual attraction, though. It will just majorly screw things up."

"Well, I don't know; I was kind of hoping . . . ."

"No Brenda; no Brenda. You gotta keep these things separate. Take it from me. I learned my lessons the hard way. I got so tired of all my roommates falling in love with me. To combat the epidemic, I even advertised for men thinking that I would be safe, but nope, same thing, even fags! Eventually, I had to adopt a rigorous screening process. I got to the point when I was interviewing prospective roommates that I would just ask them point blank, 'Are you attracted to me? I apologize for the bluntness, but it will save us both a lot of trouble in the long run.' Half of them lied anyway and ended up following me around like puppy dogs in no time, but I know that I avoided a lot of stress that way."

"I can't ask that straight out like you," Brenda protested. "I don't have enough nerve. I just hope that I get some decent responses. This would really help if it works out. Ever since Kim moved in with Kim, I've suffered financially," she said with a sour look on her face.

"Oh right. You've never suffered financially," said Meagan as she got up from the table, went to the fridge and pulled out some cranberry juice.

"Even when you were a kid, you were hoarding your allowance. You want some?"

"No, thanks. My water's good."

"You've got tons of money in the bank, Bren."

"That's savings that I don't want to touch. That's my nest egg. I have to prepare for my future. No one else is going to take care of me. I need a substantial nest egg, Meagan. I'm not going to eat dog food during my pension days like you. I'm on a strict budget these days."

"Speaking of budgets, how much does it cost to run an ad like this? I haven't had to take one out for so long now."

"You're lucky. You don't have to go through this kind of thing anymore."

"I do! I go through hell, Brenda! Changing girlfriends is the same thing, and it's a lot worse when the kind of passion that follows me around is involved. I'm not even looking for it and it finds me. The intensity level is insane."

"Okay, sorry. I just wish Kim weren't leaving. We were perfect for each other. We had adjusted to each other's habits and accepted one another's idiosyncrasies. God, why do women move in together so fast? It's too early. They barely know each other."

"That depends, Brenda. Sometimes you just have to follow your heart like Adrienne and me."

"At least you and Adrienne had known each other for a while. They did it within three weeks, not least of all because then Kim H. wouldn't have to pay rent at her old place. But I suppose it is romantic. Do you know how she and Kim met? I don't think I told you the whole story yet. They were in Pandora's and Kim H. was browsing the aisles and had taken down *Transgender Warriors* by Feinberg and was reading the inside cover. She became so engrossed that she didn't realize how long she had been standing there. Meanwhile, Kim N. had wanted to get into the same section. She had been waiting a considerably long time and had done numerous circuits around the other sections. She finally got impatient and approached Kim H. and whispered, 'I'm sorry, but I am also trying to get to the "F" section, Falaudi. Could you just move over a bit?' Kim H. was exactly in front of the part of the section that Kim N. wanted, *exactly*. So then Kim H. looks up at Kim N., sees how cute she is, and Kim N. is thinking the same thing, and it's love at first sight! Isn't that great? What if it had been 'R'? That's just fate. Why doesn't something like that ever happen to me?"

Something *had* happened to her. Something had happened eight months ago that no one would have called fate, something that wasn't romantic. Brenda was never going to tell anyone: *anyone*. She would make sure that there would never be a single thread available for unraveling - ever.

Brenda had placed a different kind of ad in two weekly papers and a monthly magazine. It was a three-month ad amongst the sparse columns of "Women Looking for Women." She left out *professional* in hopes of disguising herself. She had had seven responses, among them: one with a poem, one with unappealing, amateur nude photos from a girl and her boyfriend who "wouldn't touch you unless you wanted him to," and a letter from Lisa. Brenda had never been overly friendly with her, but they had maintained an amicable relationship after Lisa and Meagan had broken up. Though it was exasperatingly tempting to reveal this juicy story to Meagan and others, Brenda didn't. Many times the words almost came spilling, falling, gushing from her mouth, swept along in the deluge of all the others that she also had had no intention of speaking. Miraculously, Lisa's banal reply, with its very lame attempt at humor ("Dear Shy Girl, I have to say that this is my first time. For personal ads, I mean, ha ha!") was not divulged. Brenda simultaneously prevented a crippling embarrassment for Lisa and thwarted a pedigree opportunity for Meagan's cruel mockery.

Lisa had written on the purple and white lined paper her grandmother had given her for Christmas. Lilac clumps adorned the four corners, compressing the actual writing space into a thin oval. In the oval she had described herself accurately and honestly as a medium-height dirty-blonde with average looks who was interested in music and movies; someone who liked to watch sports and go camping, someone who liked romantic walks on the beach, candlelight dinners, and meaningful conversation; someone who was looking for a casual relationship leading to "whatever develops"; someone who didn't usually respond to personal ads, but thought what the hell, give it a chance; someone who was tired of the bar scene and a little lonely sometimes. That's all.

Brenda had considered burning it, holding it between her fingertips, flicking the lighter and watching the paper scorch and curl upward as far as possible before she dropped it into an ashtray. But she didn't and ended up stuffing it next to her vibrator in the back of her bottom drawer.

Two of the replies Brenda considered keepers, leaving her with a difficult choice: which one to pursue? What if she chose wrong? They both sounded promising, though correspondence could be thoroughly deceptive: remember the young Republican who wrote such beautiful poetry? Brenda pondered this decision like a Greek philosopher before choosing "Vixen" over "Heather." The eventual decisive criterion was the e-mail address. "Vixen," Brenda decided, exhibited more creativity and allure than the sensible, rather ordinary, "Heather." It was a matter of flair and style, a certain *je ne sais quoi*. So "Vixen" and Brenda continued to exchange witticisms, life tidbits, and subtle, sexual hints, and when a proper e-mail courtship period (dashed with slightly obsessive anxiety and expectation) had passed, a coffee date was set. They decided upon Scampy's restaurant at the entrance to Northwood Mall. Scampy's was a spacious, comfortable family restaurant where it was highly unlikely that they would run into anyone they knew.

"What will you be wearing?" wrote "Vixen".

"I'll be wearing a blue shirt," Brenda wrote back.

"I'll find you."

Brenda began primping early, and it was tough to keep it from Meagan. She wanted to ask her cousin about clothes. She wanted to ask her cousin about perfume and cologne. She wanted to ask her cousin about conversation. She spent forty-five minutes in the drugstore buying some new body lotion to replace the dried, cakey jar in her medicine cabinet. She rubbed the cream onto her arms and shoulders and hard into her cracked, rough elbows. She continued up and down her legs, concentrating on the ultra-sensitive inner thigh and then softly over her stomach. She lightly massaged the lotion into her breasts. She revisited the back of her neck and her buttocks, her feet and in between her toes. It was while she was rubbing the backs of her ears that she remembered the number one place to apply perfume, surely body lotion as well. She had heard it not so long ago. It took her a few minutes to remember from where, but then she recalled that it was from Julie's cute friend, Sarah. It had been at the dinner. Sarah. That was it, that cute Sarah. Sarah had quizzed them on where the number one place to apply perfume was. There were five choices: the back of the neck, behind the knees, behind the ears, the lower back, or the heel.

"What do you say, everyone? Okay, the number one answer is . . . behind the knees!" Brenda assailed behind her knees.

She bought some black "no smear" mascara and then lost sleep that she should have chosen brown. Out of her storage closet she unburied her hot pink dumbbells and puffed her way through three sets of ten with her arms burning. She used an emery board on her nails twice a day. Conscientiously, she trimmed her pubic hair with petite nail scissors. She bought a new pair of Levis that she wore around her condo every night to stretch out. She resisted getting her hair cut. It was too risky. She had suffered the anguish of enough disappointing cuts before important events and was not going to get run over by that train again. She began talking to her pillow again; stroking it again, kissing it again, feeling it up again, whispering filthy words to it again. She wrapped around and held the perfect, silent, yielding girlfriend against her tight until she fell asleep.

She arrived at seven for their seven-thirty date: dates, early; parties, late, said Meagan. She chose a table that was to the right of the center aisle and sat in the chair facing the door. She asked for two menus and an orange juice. Every time she took a sip it felt like it immediately wanted to drip out of her. She reluctantly went to the toilet twice in twenty minutes and would have gone a third time, but she dared not leave the chair after 7:20. She read the menu over and over, but couldn't have told you to this day what dishes they offered, except for orange juice and BLT's that came with fries.

At seven twenty-six a woman entered the restaurant, glanced at Brenda, and then continued to the back looking from side to side. She did the same walking back up the aisle, except this time she did not look over Brenda's way. Brenda watched the back of her blue nylon jacket as she walked out of the door. The hair, razor-cut, on the back of her neck tapered into a fresh "v."

After she could breathe again without tightness, Brenda decided that it didn't necessarily have to be "Vixen". She explained it to herself like this: Half the population had what could be considered brown hair, and she never said what she would be wearing anyway. Short cuts were not exclusively lesbian. That person hadn't necessarily exaggerated head movements when she walked out of the restaurant. It wasn't possible to convey in an instant what Brenda thought she had seen. Could an Olympian millisecond contain all that disgust and disappointment? A glance was sufficient? Could she actually justify that she didn't have to sit down to talk because she knew that she couldn't get past the non-attraction, not even a cup of coffee to see if maybe there was someone who really subscribed to that inner beauty line? Was it a microflash of an unadorned, bare cruelty where there was going to be no time wasted on a non-beneficial performance?

No, Brenda concluded. The woman that she had seen wasn't the image that she had had of "Vixen" in her head anyway. It was pure coincidence. With the real "Vixen", something had come up. Brenda waited until 8:00. "Guess I've been stood up," she said to the sympathetic waiter and then ordered a BLT with fries and ate surprisingly cheerfully.

* * * *

Meagan stroked the hair around Adrienne's ear and wedged her knee in tighter between her legs. They were out of a candlelight bath and were now lying in bed. Meagan was very proud of her wrought iron bed. It was the second stop on her apartment tour, after the shower. There were iron half-circles at each end supported by rods, with four medium-length posts at the corner. Meagan liked to say that the posts were for bondage, but really only one of her girlfriends had acquiesced so far, looking-for-romance-Lisa.

"There's a lot of history in this bed. Herstory too." Meagan smiled, pleased at her delivery of what she considered original wit. "I told you that this bed used to belong to Eric from Moods Hair, right? Lots of women; I'm talking lots of women. And just like Hockey Night in Canada, the tradition continues. Boy, if this bed could talk. Anyway, speaking of herstory, I want to know more about Julie in bed. I can't imagine it really. Yuuuuuuck!"

"Meeeeeagan!" Adrienne ignored her and slid her hands under Meagan's tee shirt. "We've already been over this."

"What? I'm just curious. What kind of toys? Be more specific. You've never been specific. Who did what to whom? Details, give me details."

"Not now, Meagan," she said and began kissing Meagan's stomach.

"Did you strap it on for her, too? Oh, that feels good. It's a psychological thing, you know."

"Meagan, I really don't feel like talking about Julie and my former sex life right now, if you don't mind." She continued her deliberate kissing.

"Okay, forget it. Later. Tell me again about the first time that you saw me in your office and what you thought of me."

"I'll have to stop what I'm doing now to do that. Is that really what you want?"

"I'll temporarily sacrifice it . . . temporarily."

Adrienne stopped kissing and moved back up to the top of the bed. "I've already told you a million times," she said as she grabbed Meagan's chin and squeezed it.

"Tell me again. I like to hear it," Meagan said with what she believed to be an irresistible, sexy pout.

"Okay," relented Adrienne. "I wondered why you were there, of course, but I especially wondered why you were there with Brenda. I had seen you two at the bar before and didn't think that you were a couple, so it was odd to see you at a tax office together. I didn't know she was your cousin then."

Meagan sat up suddenly. "It doesn't come across that she's my girlfriend, does it?"

"No, no, no, no. I never thought that. Relax," said Adrienne as she snuggled back up to Meagan and tried to get her to recline again to recapture the interrupted mood.

"Whew, good. That's a relief." She slid back down.

"What's wrong with anyone thinking that Brenda's your girlfriend anyway?"

"Oh, please."

"Come on, Meagan. I like your cousin. She's kinda cute. She's definitely unique. She just needs to loosen up a little, find someone to have fun with. In fact, if we weren't going out, I wouldn't mind dating her myself."

Meagan looked terror-stricken. "Don't even joke about that! You are joking, right?"

"Maybe I am, and maybe I'm not," she taunted. "By the way, did you two finish the ad? I sure hope she finds someone good to live with."

"I don't want to talk about Brenda anymore. It's ruining the mood. Omitting anything about her, continue. What else did you think of me?"

"I thought you were so sexy."

Adrienne put her arm across Meagan's stomach and pulled her close so that she could rest her head on her shoulder.

"And . . . ."

"Well, I wanted to find out why you were there and help you with it, of course."

"And . . . ." Meagan urged impatiently.

"Meagan! You know all of this already. And I was so disappointed that I had to deal exclusively with Brenda. Sorry, have to use her name. I wanted to deal with you. I wanted to drink you in."

"And what else? Be more specific."

Adrienne tried to wiggle away now, but now Meagan had a very tight grip on her so she became still.

"And I thought that you had beautiful hands. I tried to imagine everything that your hands did all day. Put on a ring; open a door; turn on the television . . . ."

"Play with myself?"

"Yes, even that. And I imagined those same precious hands all over me. I wanted them holding mine, warm and safe. Then it was your beautiful eyes. I wanted to see what you had seen, learn what you had learned. What images had come to you during the day, during your lifetime? I wanted to know what programs and movies you had watched so that I could know a part of you through them. It would be exciting to watch something that I knew you had seen. I wanted the same images entering us. That was the only way we could connect that early.

What about me? What did you think about me?"

"I thought you were hot."

"And . . . ."

"I was surprised because I certainly didn't expect to find someone like you at a tax office. I was just tagging along with Brenda, expecting to be bored. I was totally unprepared for you that day. But that's what they say, when you least expect it."

"And what else? Be more specific."

"And I thought your breasts were perfect."

"And . . . ." Adrienne wiggled back and softly kissed Meagan on the cheek. "You still think they're perfect?"

* * * *

"Wow, she is hot," Meagan had said to Brenda as they left the tax office. "I didn't know she worked there."

"Yeah, she is pretty," agreed Brenda.

"Wow, am I glad that I decided to hang out with you today! Why did you suddenly start getting your taxes done here for anyway? Why did you switch, and why didn't you tell me about her before?"

"I wasn't totally satisfied with my other place, and so my colleague recommended them. I never thought about telling you."

"What a lucky break for me. It's fate. It's the direct result of one of those hundreds of tiny, seemingly insignificant decisions that we make everyday, Brenda. Do I hurry for the light or wait? Do I stop to browse or not? Where do I decide to have coffee today? Do I listen to the end of the song before leaving the house, or do I just leave? Try to retrace each distinct step of some of your history sometime, Brenda. It's mind-boggling. You meet or miss your destiny by seconds, by whims, yours and other people's. Do I go with Brenda or not? I had no reason to come with you today, except that I was bored. Sorry. Fate led me here. This is definitely my new project. Okay, when do you have to go back to pick up the returns?"

"Meeeeegaan, she has a girlfriend."

"Like that matters. Who? What's her name? Do I know her?"

"Julie Bell."

"That loser? No way."

"Way. They've been going out almost two years or something."

"No way. How does that useless human being score someone like Adrienne?"

"You haven't seen them together at Rumors?"

"Maybe, I can't remember. Remember I'm not always in my best shape at Rumors."

"I don't know anything about her except that she works in her father's tax office, and she's Julie Bell's girlfriend," said Brenda with a frown. She walked sulkily ahead of her cousin into the parking lot and around to the passenger door. This was the disapproval treatment she gave Meagan for not concentrating solely on *their* conversation. Brenda's entire body clenched with irritation and her head throbbed with a pounding emotional headache. Meagan had become so inured to the treatment that she barely noticed anymore.

"You can get Julie's credit report through work, right Bren?"

"Right."

Meagan unlocked the doors and they climbed up and into the black Explorer. "Check up on her for me, will you?"

"Sure."

Meagan turned the key in the ignition, put on her sunglasses, and shoved in a "Rap Mix" cassette. "So, how am I going to do this?"

"I don't know."

"I'm not asking you. I'm thinking aloud."

"Well, you might want to ask me," said Brenda with a satisfied look now that she was again maneuvering herself to the forefront of the conversation.

Meagan rested her foot lightly on the gas but didn't put it into gear. She looked at her cousin. "Why might I want to ask you?"

"You might want to ask me because I might know something."

"Because you might know something like what?"

"Because I might know something like there is a women-who-love-women dinner planned by a one Julie Bell. I saw the ad last week. See, you miss stuff by not reading those ads, Meagan."

"I fucking love you, Cuz," she said and pinched Brenda's cheek. She thrust the Explorer into reverse and squealed out of the parking space. "Trust me; it won't be hard to get her away from that loser. Once we get her past the initial guilt, it will be a piece of cake."

* * * *

Between long kisses Meagan continued, "That dinner at the Italian restaurant was practically unbearable. The whole time I was talking to Brenda I never heard a word that she said, which is really nothing new anyway. All my concentration was focused on trying to listen to what they were saying at your table. I was paranoid to even look over there. I didn't know if you had figured out that I had sent the flowers or not. You barely noticed me and I was in anguish."

"Of course I noticed you. I was pretty sure that it was you, but I couldn't say anything. I was feeling guilty as hell, and I hadn't even done anything yet. God, it was so hard not to stare over at you all night."

"Bell watches everything like a hawk, and I felt like she could read and intercept everything that was meant for you, all the messages that I was sending you with my eyes."

"I got them."

"And she has that permanent zit on the side of her nose. I can barely look at her. It's just hard for me to understand what you saw in her. I was already dying for you. Thank god for Tracey so I didn't have to wait too long after that to get things rolling. I like to call her the Switzerland of friends." Meagan smiled. "Neutral. Won't stand in the way of passion, that girl. I owe her a lot for being the intermediary. I already wanted to fuck you so badly that night and yet I had to imagine you going home with her. Do you know how hard that was for me?"

"I'm sorry, baby." Adrienne stroked her cheek gently.

"Passion. I need passion. I can't survive without passion. You never had passion with Julie. This is passion. What about our first coffee? Tell me about that again, too."

"I thought you were beautiful," said Adrienne. She began kissing and sucking Meagan's ear. "And you wore that green Calvin Klein shirt -- and you were so nervous and handsome, couldn't take my eyes off you."

"My spirit needs passion. I can't be held back." Meagan stared intensely into Adrienne's eyes. "You're so beautiful. Why do you love me? You could have anyone you want, why me? Her eyes filled with tears. "What are you doing with me? Tell me. I have to know. Why me?"

Chapter 6 – Ballpark

Julie picked up the telephone receiver, held it for a while and then replaced it on the cradle. She stared at the phone. Her heart pounded. She took a deep breath and picked it back up, dialed half a number this time and then quickly hung up. Jeezus, come on for Christ's sake! She picked it up again, pressed it against her chest, and then hung up. She picked it up again, dialed the full number and then slammed it down before it rang. Jeezus! She grabbed it and dialed.

On the second ring Meagan said, "Hello."

Second ring. Wasn't prepared, was expecting third or fourth, didn't give her enough time. Damn it! Why did she have to answer? Quick, think fast.

"Oh, I am zo zorey, zis iz zee wrong number," said Julie in her best French chef's accent and then hung up. She knew that she should have waited longer but was only able to last twenty minutes before she called again.

"Hello," said Meagan abruptly.

Fuck.

"Hi, Meagan. It's Julie. May I speak to Adrienne, please?" she said innocently.

"Hold on," said Meagan tentatively and tersely.

After a long delay, Adrienne answered. "Hello, Julie. Did you just call here a little while ago?"

"No, why?"

"You didn't just call here and do a pathetic imitation of a French accent and then hang up?"

"No."

"Are you sure?"

"Yes."

"All right. Forget it then. What do you want?"

"Fine, thanks. And you?"

"What do you want, Julie? And why are you calling here at ten o'clock at night?"

Accompanying the disintegration of love is the painful rearranging of the boundaries. She used to be able to call at two a.m. to say that she loved her or that the world was closing in. Now she couldn't call past ten.

"I want to talk to you. I want to see you."

"Why? There's nothing to say. It's over, Julie. Haven't you accepted that yet?"

"There's a lot to say, Adrienne. I haven't seen you yet. It's hard to accept by a note. By proxy. I need to see you face-to-face."

"I don't want to see you. Isn't that obvious?" Meagan stood right next to Adrienne like a coach.

"I need to see you."

"Julie, I can't."

"Where's the person I know? Almost two years we were together, and then you left. You were too cowardly to show your face, and I let you go. I let you take everything you wanted without dispute. I didn't rip up your clothes. I didn't wait under the bed when you came to get your stuff. I easily could have, but why give your new friends more ammunition? I want to have dinner with you. That is all. I think you owe me that. Were you ever planning to see me?"

"Should I play back the answering machine for you, Julie? We saved it. The, 'You fucking cunts! You pieces of shit. You deserve to burn in hell. You're both dead.' Should I play that for you?"

"That was just after you left. It was that freak storm in May when all the trees and poles went down and the power went out. Talk about an omen. Couldn't even go outside for a walk. You wouldn't have done better. What if the shoe were on the other foot? How would you have reacted? Calm and dignified, right? Well, it's easy to say when it's just theoretical. You have no idea, Adrienne, no idea. Anyway, I've had time to cool down. Isn't that what you were waiting for? I've got some pictures of yours, and I have the phone bill to show you what you owe."

"You can mail them."

"I want to see you. You took almost two years. Please give me two hours back. Please."

Julie remembered a television interview with a famous defense lawyer. "Never ask a witness a question that you don't already know the answer to."

"Don't you want your tape back?"

"Let me think it over and I'll get back to you."

* * * *

"Saaaaaaaaarah, what am I gonna wear!" Julie yelled from her bedroom.

"I'm trying to read, Julie. Hey, listen to this about this guy. Posing as a Hasidic Jew, he bilked major financial institutions all over the world out of millions of dollars. I can't even get a credit card! I remember on *Larry King* there was this famous treasurer or former president of the World Bank or whatever. He was talking about how it's easier to borrow ten million dollars than it is to borrow a thousand. The crooks get all the money. People want to *give* them money. Unsolicited, with these atrocious credit ratings, they are mailed credit cards. Unbelievable!"

Julie stomped into the living room where Sarah was reading a newspaper.

"That's fascinating, Sarah. Now this is important. You have to help me. *What* am I going to wear?"

"Calm down, Julie. It's Adrienne. She already knows what you look like. There are no surprises here."

"That's what I mean. She's seen all my clothes before."

"It's not a date, Julie."

"I *know* that. Do you have to take the pleasure out of absolutely every little thing?"

"I'm just trying to help. What'd you invite me over for anyway?"

July 26th. Nothing else mattered but July 26th. Julie looked at the other banal and meaningless numbers below the kittens on the calendar page, but the 26th was bold with life. It spoke to her. Had she been a Christian, it would have told her to kill in Jesus' name.

Adrienne had called Wednesday night around nine. "Hi, Julie. I've got some time on Tuesday the 26th. I can meet you for coffee at about 6:30. How about the Food Fair in the Sears Mall?"

"Okay. No dinner? Oh, never mind. That's all right. Food Fair's fine. Where should we meet?"

"How about the main entrance? Bring the tape."

"Sure, looking forward to it, too. See you at 6:30 on the 26th."

Julie went back into her room and tore the shirt off. She threw it violently into the pile on the floor. She yanked the closet door open again and glared at her wardrobe. Nothing looked right. It was fiercely disturbing to her that without discrimination she had worn all these clothes regularly. They all looked lousy.

She turned back to the mirror and tried to smooth her short brown hair down at the sides. She crushed her palms into the side of her head and held them there.

"God, what did I get my hair cut for? Jeeezus Christ, she made a fucking mess of it! No time to grow back." She pawed her head wildly. How could anyone so ugly go anywhere? Where was the gel? Now what was wrong with her face? Who would kiss her? Who could imagine it? This was the last time that she was going to go to Jennifer. She didn't care if she was hot and her nail polish matched her shoes. She never did what she was told, only what she wanted.

Julie tried to brush off her rage and smile her best smile into the mirror. Remember, like the soaps if you could with a controlled half-whisper and irresistibly sensual now. "Oh, hello, Adrienne. Looks like the years have been good to you." Weeks--didn't sound right with weeks.

"Saaaaaaarah! You got something I can borrow?"

"My stuff's too small for you, Julie," she yelled back. "And I don't have time to go home and get anything anyway. You've got lots of nice stuff. Wear the black sweater. It looks good."

As Julie pulled on another pair of jeans she noticed how unsightly the roll of fat around her stomach had become. Her unattended pubic hair grew unrestrained all the way down her thighs to her knees. *Dear Abby, My friend has an embarrassing problem . . . .*

She picked up a rumpled, black crewneck out of the pile and tried it on again. "Black is the safest, and she hasn't seen this sweater. She likes black."

"Sarah?" she yelled.

"What?"

"In minutes, how much time a week do you figure that you are happy?"

"I don't know. Don't bug me. I'm reading. Get dressed."

"Come on, how many? Or in a day, that's easier. How many minutes have you been truly happy today?"

"I'd be truly happy if you wouldn't talk to me right now."

"Oh come on. I figure that I've been happy, really happy, for less than four minutes in the last two and a half months. The only time was on Wednesday night when Adrienne called."

Julie walked back into the living room. "Okay, how does this look?"

"Good. This isn't a reunion, you know. Don't get your hopes up."

"I'm not, and don't be so negative. Jeez, negative, negative, negative, and you call me the pessimistic one. Can't I experience a little happiness here and there? Is that too much to ask? What I am saying is that they were rare minutes of pure happiness, unadulterated. It's frightening if we compare these minutes to the minutes that we're not. Hours we're not actually. So, that's twenty-four hours in a day and sixty minutes per hour, that's sixty times twenty-four . . . ."

"Julie, I am trying to read. Finish getting dressed!"

"Okay, but just think about it sometime. It'll frighten your little socks off. Think of your and d.dee's case. Oh god, what pants am I going to wear?"

Time is so disproportionate in the romantic sphere. The time spent moping and scheming compared with actual moments spent contentedly together. A month spent waiting for a call and then maybe a four-hour date, tops, in return. Yet this inequality is acceptable. Our emotional systems become overloaded with someone we've seen only for sixty minutes. Suddenly our entire existence depends solely on someone we've known for only twelve point five hours. Four minutes and we are contemplating suicide, two minutes, marriage. Or conversely, a three-minute phone call can sustain us for eight weeks; a life can collapse in 16,296 hours.

Julie arrived at the Sears Mall forty minutes early, so she browsed hyperactively. Minutes felt like those mammoth concrete pillars that held up suspension bridges. If anyone had ever asked her to describe the closest to a palpable madness that she had ever felt, she would have described it as physically counting those interminable minutes.

When she and Adrienne had started dating, she used to arrive early just so that she could wait and saturate herself in the exquisite anticipation, twenty or thirty precious extra minutes of happiness. Julie wrote a poem during one of those waits. Well, you couldn't exactly have called it a poem; it didn't rhyme or anything, but she liked it, folded it up, and tucked it into her zippered Bible that she'd kept from long ago summer church camp. Nobody would look in there.

You don't know it yet, but I call you a Saint. Because of you, I remember meanings of words. Like freedom, like joy. I am ashamed to admit what you're capable of, ashamed of the emptiness until you appear. I can't take you in all at once. I think about you only a little at a time, in increments. If I didn't ease into you, I would leave this earth. For days I could wait here. You look different now. Much different than the first time. I watch our love all over you now. I transformed your body. Did you transform mine? For months I didn't even know what kind of shoes you wore because I watched only your face.

After the pool night (Sarah had prevented her from calling as soon as they got home from the bar that evening), Julie had descended into her incapacitated/obsessive stage (Should I do a workshop on that, d.dee?). From seconds after she awoke in the morning until she pulled the covers up at night, it was like she chanted a steady mantra of "Adrienne, Adrienne, Adrienne."

She had the number, but when was best to call? How much time was it appropriate to wait? She wanted to appear neither desperate nor disinterested. She also had to consider letting Adrienne call first. Sarah cautioned her that she should be a little less eager than usual.

"I thought that women liked to be chased."

"Chased is correct, Julie, not smothered. I say this as a friend."

Julie waited four impatient, anxiety-ridden days and then left a message on Adrienne's answering machine. Because she was so nervous, she was relieved that Adrienne wasn't home.

Leaving a message was preferable to fumbling and stuttering her way through a call. "Hi, Adrienne. This is Julie. From the bar last Friday, remember? I was just wondering if you'd like to do something, if you aren't busy sometime. Give me a call if you get a chance. Bye."

Then she took the telephone off the stand and set it at her feet for the rest of the evening while she watched television, while she stared at the television. When it rang, she waited until the fourth ring to answer in hopes that it would disguise any traces of her sitting there tense with the phone at her feet waiting for it to ring.

"Hello," she tried to say as nonchalantly as possible.

"Did you call her?" asked Sarah. Julie's spirits plunged like a roller coaster.

"Jeezus, Sarah! What are you doing tying up my line?"

"Yup, you called, and obviously someone hasn't called you back yet, either."

"Anything else?"

"Well, you don't have to be so rude. I'm just interested. Okay, I'm hanging up now."

Julie suffered through half of prime time and then the phone rang again.

"Mrs. Bell?"

"Ms."

"Oh, I am sorry, Ms. Bell. You do sound younger. And how are you this evening?"

"Fine."

"That's great, Ms. Bell. I am wondering if you are familiar with the Outreach Program of the Greater Vancouver Burn Unit."

"Ummmmm, well, I've heard of it, I think." How could anyone hang up on the Burn Unit?

"Oh good. Don't worry. You're like most people, Ms. Bell. You've heard of us; the name is floating around in your head, but you still can't quiiiiiiite place us, and so what I am here to do is to keep the public informed, which is really the essence of what we do. What we are is just an extension of the Unit, and what we provide is the crucial out-patient support that the victims so desperately need after they leave the hospital. I assume that you are well aware of the great stigma attached to being a burn victim, Ms. Bell."

"Yes."

The telemarketer, trained like a marathon runner to need only a Dixie Cup of water splashed in her face without losing her pace, breathed at the designated intervals and continued her run flawlessly. "We have done an awful lot of work to raise our profile on behalf of the scarred victims, including many children. So we are getting out there and contacting the kind, supportive people in our community, because as I am sure that you can imagine, Ms. Bell, the cost of reintegration is by no means cheap, and that's where generous people like you . . . ."

Julie hung up on the Burn Unit and felt like a sneaky lowlife. "That should be against the law, calling me in my own home." She took the phone to the kitchen when she made a ham sandwich; she left it just outside the open bathroom door when she took a bath, and at eleven p.m., she called Sarah back apologetically.

"What if she lost the matchbook, Sarah? Those are easy to lose. I have before. I didn't leave my number on the machine. So, what if she is sitting there right now going crazy because she wants to call but doesn't have my number? . . . Well, maybe she won't think to look in the phone book; I might not. Why didn't I leave my number on the machine just in case? Do you think I should call back? . . . Why not?"

She put the phone under her bed praying to wake up to Adrienne's middle-of-the-night hunger. Couldn't she be the cause of insomnia for once? Couldn't she soothe those demons of darkness for anyone? Just let her try. The call didn't come that night. It came the next evening at 7:12. It was late, but it stroked her with relief.

On their first date (at Sarah's insistence), they went to a movie. They went to the 7:20 showing of *From Here to Eternity* at the Paradise Theatre on Granville Street. After the movie, they went to Lavender's for coffee and discussed how movies had changed. Was it for the better or not? Was it better to have evolved to the point of graphic sex, or was it better to watch couples hugging, not pressed against each other in any meaningful way? A whorehouse or a social club, shucks instead of fuck? Couples with twin beds or sadomasochism? These were the invaluable hours when you began to reveal yourselves, the exquisite times when you couldn't wait for one another again. But it doesn't last long. The cocoon eventually opens and the butterfly flies away.

* * * *

"I was so wrong, Julie. Could you ever find it in your heart to forgive me? Please, please, please take me back. I'll do anything for you. Meagan doesn't deserve to kiss your feet. She's lousy in bed. She only works out her arms, you know. Please take me back. I love you, and I made a horrible, terrible mistake." That's what she'll say, Julie imagined.

She never said any of it.

Adrienne came in a white, short-sleeved blouse. You could imagine her putting it on and buttoning herself up; her chin bent, hair falling into her eyes.

"Hello, Julie. You're looking well." She didn't come familiarly close.

"No, I'm not," Julie replied.

"When did you start wearing hats?"

"I'm trying to change my life. You look well; you always did with a tan."

"Thanks. You want a coffee? I'll buy."

They sat on the uncomfortable, white plastic chairs that resembled outdoor patio furniture.

"Do we really need these umbrellas inside? How's work? How's your dad?" Julie asked.

"The same. He can relax now. Tax season's over. The phone hardly rings anymore. I read magazines for most of the day, the usual. We did have a bizarre incident this season, though."

"What was that?"

"One of our new clients, this Melanie Patterson, brought in five years' worth of receipts in shoeboxes. She hadn't filed in four years and of course expected us to unravel chaos. Oh, you would have loved her stuff, Julie. The profile you could have built."

"Hotel, Prozac, Chiropractic?"

"Yup, all of it. You would have had a field day." Adrienne spoke precisely and almost as charmingly as she had in the early days. Only this time the consequence of not maintaining the level of frivolity was much more severe. So she laughed and she joked--anything to delay what was under the surface.

"Ross worked really hard on it, but when she came to pick up the returns, she refused to pay. She said the fee was too high, so we kept them. Then the next week she came back. I was suspicious and uncomfortable, but what could I do? I couldn't throw her out of the office. She demanded to see Ross, who was hiding downstairs in his office. The returns were out on the counter, and I half-turned to call him when she grabbed them and headed for the door! I'm pretty quick, and thank god the door was only half-open, so I grabbed Melanie and pulled her down. I was in a skirt, too."

"No way."

"Way. Her boyfriend was outside in the getaway car. Ross heard all of this and finally came upstairs to see what was going on. Dad was out with a client and missed the whole thing. I was on top of her, and she was flailing at me. She kept screaming, 'I'll sue you! I'll sue you! Call the police! Help! Somebody call the police!' By this time her boyfriend had abandoned Plan A and started up the walk. Ross went out to head him off, and they also ended up on the ground. Now the boyfriend's screaming, too, and Ross has him in a headlock. She's screaming for the police, and he's screaming, 'No, no, not the police. I'm still on parole, you bitch.' People from the offices across the street were watching out the windows. It was pretty embarrassing."

"I can't believe it! So, what happened?"

"The police came and broke it up. I'm not sure if they were arrested or not, but they took them away in the police car. I don't know what's going to happen now. The returns have been impounded as evidence."

"No! Really? How much was Ross's fee?"

"It was only $1,400. That's reasonable. He did a lot of work. He could have charged much more."

"Shit. Burn the returns, and let her take her shoeboxes to someone else."

"I wish I could. Can you believe that we might have to go to court over this?"

"I'd like to get my hands on those shoeboxes."

They were getting along so well, but it was now the end of the preamble. Adrienne sat staring at her hands before she began.

"I wish I could think of a good segue from shoeboxes, Julie, but I can't. I know that you won't believe me, but I never wanted to hurt you. I'm sorry. I am so sorry. I wanted to tell you that before, but I had to give you time. Understandably you were hurting. You needed time to cool down."

"Hurting? I was white hot." Julie said in a very low voice. Adrienne closed her eyes.

Julie squeezed her coffee cup with both hands. "You didn't go it alone, Adrienne. You had someone to talk you through it. Someone to help you dissect every one of my character flaws."

"That's not what we were doing."

"You never went to bed lonely. You slept comforted through the night while I was lucky if I could get fifteen minutes at a time."

"It wasn't that easy, Julie. Besides, you had Sarah."

"That's not the same and you know it!"

Adrienne looked around to see if anybody was watching them. "Julie, come on. Let's not fight here. I still don't know if meeting you was a good idea. Sometimes you scare me. But you're right. I owe you that. Can't we be friends in time?"

"I have enough friends. Why?"

Adrienne looked at her hands a long time again before she spoke. "I'm just not in love with you anymore. That's all. I'm so sorry."

This was the conversation that they should have had two months ago. This was the fight that should have erupted with fresh, searing anger, not with these watered-down, delayed emotions. Julie had already been knocked out. She had managed to get up feebly, and all she was doing now was trying to get in a few futile jabs before collapsing again. Adrienne had forced her to be on her best behaviour to even get the opportunity to have the fight. Adrienne had counted on a subdued reaction. It felt so frustratingly wrong to Julie. She was having this cold conversation with a person she had been so intimate with. It was a hell that felt all too--and not at all--real.

"Why?"

"Jules, don't."

"Could you just give me a hint, then, about what's so wrong with me? A general idea, ballpark, you know, so that I can improve myself for my next girlfriend?"

"Julie, it's not you. It's me. Don't blame yourself. I'm the one who changed. That's all. Don't make me do this. You can easily get someone better than me. You deserve more."

"Speaking of girlfriends, how's your new one by the way?"

"She's fine. You know, Julie, if you just gave her a chance, you'd like her. She's not what people think. You'd be surprised. She's changed dramatically. She used to be so full of herself, but she's not anymore.

People misunderstand her because they don't know her. Once you get close to her, once you get past all the defenses, you find a totally different person."

"You mean like Jekyll and Hyde?"

"Can't you give her the benefit of the doubt?"

"It's too early to ask that of me, Adrienne. Aren't you being a touch insensitive and premature? And why should I when she has never given it to anyone else in her entire life? If she were an animal, what kind would she be?"

"Jules . . . ."

"What kind? A snake?"

"I'm not answering you."

"Forget it. I don't want to know."

"Do you know about Louise's party, Julie?"

"Yeah."

"Why don't you come, then? We're gonna be there. Why don't we break the ice? In our community, it's inevitable that we're going to run into each other from time to time, so we may as well make it as comfortable as possible. You and Meagan are going to have to face one another one day."

Julie realized that she was going to hear none of what she had invented and she felt her stomach slide away with her hope. One more time her script was being rewritten right in front of her and she wasn't holding the pen. Years of thwarted plans might have deterred another woman, but Julie never gave up her scheming and dreaming. Why, when the surface was usually misleading? If you could survive the perilous dig out of convention and conformity, you would find infinite possibilities.

You would make thunderous mistakes, but you never gave up writing your scripts. If you did that, you were the living dead. She remembered trying to explain this many times to Adrienne who never seemed to scheme for anything. Julie concluded that it was because Adrienne was the kind of woman who lived just fending off those schemes.

"I'll think about the party," she said to Adrienne.

* * * *

"She looked so beautiful," Julie told Sarah the next day. She set her iced mocha on the table and wiped her mouth with the serviette. "She kept talking about how much Meagan has changed. I believe people can change, Sarah, but I don't believe *she* can change. She can change her hair; she can change the way she drives to work, but she cannot change the essence of her being. I am surprised that I remained so calm. I thought there might be a blow up, but really I felt too weak. Adrienne thinks it would be good if I came to Louise's party. I don't know. What do you think?"

"I think you should go. Adrienne's right. You're going to have to go out and show yourself at one of these parties sometime, and this is as good a starting point as any."

"Yeah, but everyone there is going to know the situation. They all know what Meagan did . . . ."

"What *Adrienne* and Meagan did; you let her off like she has done nothing. She's culpable too, you know."

"All right, what *they* did. Either way, people are going to be staring and laughing or pitying me."

"No, they're not. Sure, everybody finds out surface details in lightning speed, but they don't care as much as you think they do. Believe it or not, Julie, not everyone in the world is thinking about you. They're too busy worrying about themselves. Do you know how fast gossip evaporates? I'm sorry, but you are getting to be old news. You're waaaaaaaaaaaaaay too self-centered."

"Everyone knows that Adrienne dumped me for Meagan, Sarah. They're going to know particulars too, take sides and stuff. Everyone loves to gossip, even if they don't call it that."

"It's rarely as bad as you think, Julie."

This time it was as bad as she thought, Julie wanted to tell her. The only reason that she could talk about it like this was because she had had time. She had had that proverbial time to heal. Adrienne and Meagan didn't need it. They had escaped into their rapture. They didn't have to get over anything, pull themselves up, get on with their lives, and keep their chins up. Out of their mouths streamed glib, pretty phrases, and nothing was disrupted. There's the magician who pulls out the tablecloth from under the set table, leaving the dishes, glasses, and cutlery, everything intact. Meagan in a drycleaned tux was the magician this time. She pulled out the tablecloth, but everything on Julie's table went flying: red wine, silverware, water glasses. Julie's life went flying, and Meagan stood there untouched, admiring her work. Every dark place was just as bad as Julie had imagined. She could only push it away for so long, but then it came back strangling her. She wrote another poem when she thought she had truly experienced the meaning of the words *humiliation* and *devastation* and *betrayal.* Those girls had given her the most acute vocabulary lesson of her life.

* * * *

The day after she and Brenda had visited Tessier, Brown & Associates, Meagan sent twelve, long-stemmed red roses to the office. *"A Secret Admirer,"* she had written on the card. "Do you think she'll know, Brenda?"

"Yeah, I think so."

"She was looking at me, wasn't she?"

"Yeah, she was looking at you, Meagan."

Adrienne ecstatically received the flowers with a heart full of resurgent love for Julie. "Isn't she sweet?" she murmured while opening the long, smooth, waxy-white box. *"A Secret Admirer"?* Adrienne had been in enough relationships that she had wisely adopted the "honesty-is-not-always-the-best-policy" stance. She preferred the "they-say-they-can-handle-it-but-they-can't-handle-it-so-don't-open-your-mouth" stance.

As soon as she got home that evening, Adrienne knew conclusively that Julie hadn't sent them. Had Julie sent them, she would have greeted her at the door and followed Adrienne around from room to room, all in an apparently spontaneous manner while waiting for her to mention it. And if Adrienne didn't bring it up, there were plenty of ways to work it into the conversation. Sarah's birthday was coming up and she had no idea what to get her. How long had they been going out now? You wouldn't believe what that romantic Kim did for Kim's birthday. Julie would be bursting for Adrienne's reaction had she sent the flowers. She always burst, always. She couldn't conceal surprises. She couldn't just buy a present or send a letter; she had to reveal that she had done so. If not exactly what was coming, then at least the fact that something was on the way; "You're gonna be happy next week." Often she vowed that this was the time that she would reform her old ways and keep a secret, like every year when she vowed to get her Christmas shopping done early by picking up those bargains in July. "You will never catch me at Wal-Mart on Christmas Eve again." She vowed that she wanted to learn how to enjoy the discipline of restraint for once. Each time she broke that vow. So when Adrienne walked in the door and with only a slight turn of her head Julie said, "Hi, hon," then Adrienne knew that the twelve, velvety, dark-red roses were not from the girl seated on the sofa engrossed in a soap opera.

Chapter 7 - Sent My Poems to k.d. lang

"So, who is going to be there again?" Julie asked Sarah as they approached the front door of Louise's building.

"I told you already and I don't know who else. Just relax. It will be okay."

"We should be forwarded guest lists in advance. Carol and Marla. Did you say Carol and Marla? I can't remember."

"No, I think they're in Hawaii."

"Good. Not to be rude or anything, but they drive me crazy the way they are always all over each other."

"You're just envious."

"Of that? No, I'm not. You've seen them."

"Yeah, I know. It's a little too much."

"It's uncomfortable going out with them. Even at our own parties it's hard to take. I remember last winter when we went to the Canucks' Game. I will never go anywhere in public with them again. Never. We took the Sky Train and they were hanging off each other, necking and petting, cooing pookywooky baby talk. Everyone was staring at us, and there was me, the third wheel, wishing I had stayed home watching TV with Adrienne."

Sarah started laughing.

"It's not funny."

"Sorry, but I can just imagine it."

"It's staged affection. No one's getting a look at tenderness unrehearsed. It's contrived."

Sarah giggled some more.

"Shut up."

Sarah started laughing so hard that she shook.

"It's a show! They're doing it to shock. It's not sexy at all. It's unbearable to watch."

Sarah tried to take a breath. "I know," she said. "But I can just imagine you sitting there."

They took the stairs to Louise's floor and walked down to her door. Julie knocked lightly.

"Ring the bell, Julie."

She knocked louder. No one came. Sarah reached around her and rang the bell.

"Maybe they didn't hear it, Julie. Try the door. Is it open?" Julie turned the knob and pushed the door open. She peeked into Louise's apartment.

Sarah nudged her from behind. "Go in, it's okay, go in."

"Come on in, ladies. Thought I heard something," said Louise as she appeared in the entrance. Louise was grace under pressure personified. She wore neat and comfortable simple, cotton Indian blouses, cashmere turtlenecks, or woolen vests. Her long, light-brown hair was dusted with a gray tint that she moaned about, but it reflected the light more beautifully than any artificial highlight. She was an immaculate hostess, her home always permeated by the soothing calmness of wicker and plants. She was encyclopedic about ingenious, inexpensive household hints. You obediently followed Louise as in her head she sewed and hung curtains for you, painted trim and borders, strung lights and rearranged furniture. Nothing in heaven or on earth could distract you when Louise suggested moving your coffee table or switching the bookcase and television stand. Couldn't sew? No problem, you just bought colored sheets and strung them up with hooks and clothespins. Chaos did not enter Lousie's domain.

"Wow, umbrella handles! What a great way to hang plants. I never would have thought of that," said Sarah.

"Me neither. Magazine," said Louise.

"It always looks so great in here."

"Thanks."

Julie's eyes were immediately pulled to Meagan even before her mind firmly registered that she was sitting there. It was the first sighting since the treachery. She was sitting there arrogantly. She certainly didn't look *totally changed*. She was slightly reclined in an easy chair with Adrienne on her lap. One arm was around Adrienne's waist while the other protected a beer bottle on the arm of the chair. Her feet lay comfortably across a rectangular, green velvet footstool, with her maroon and gray, Levi-socked toes curled blissfully into each other.

Meagan's mind, however, had firmly registered that Julie was now in the room, and she burst into laughter and pounded the beer bottle into the chair arm like she had just heard the joke of the century. If she was anything in film, thought Julie, she was an actress. Brenda's remarks moments before hadn't been that humorous, but now that Julie had arrived they were hysterically funny.

They could have been funny. They could have been funny if Brenda wasn't the one delivering them, if they hadn't already been horribly overworked. Practically everyone in the front room had already heard at least one variation of the routine: *Brenda's Theory of Relationships.*

"Sort of a doomsday relationship clock, if you will." Her theory was that the clock was activated the second that you met someone you were interested in. At that instant of the highest, purest, unblemished attraction, the milliseconds started whipping away in a downhill countdown to the wrenching time when you despised each other. Every phone call, every love letter, every shared opinion, every cute note, every dreamy dinner, every smile, every hand-holding in the movies, every bouquet of flowers, every getaway drive down the coast, and every anecdote did not strengthen the romance, but by striking contrast, pushed the hands toward midnight. How then did we draw this process out? How did we lengthen and maximize the courtship? How did we not go from blissfully asking, "Show me your signature" to "I fucking hate the way you brush your teeth!"

Brenda worked as a financial consultant in an investment banking firm. She was one of the first women to hold such a position in her company, an achievement that did not go unmentioned within the first five minutes whenever Meagan and Brenda met new people. Brenda's peculiar, defiant timidity, which was the cornerstone of her business success, diminished significantly however when she was with Meagan, who absorbed all her abilities and paraded them as attributes of her own imagined glamour. Beside her cousin, Brenda could only exude a paler, supporting arrogance.

d.dee sat next to Brenda, who sat at the end of the couch beside Meagan's armchair, and hers was the first voice that Julie heard distinctly. Military experts will tell you that it is the voice of your enemy that you should heed over the voice of your allies. "And so now I am looking for a place to exhibit my collages," said d.dee. "I've been working on them for about three years, and I think the ones that I did during the famine conference are the most powerful. Does anybody know where I might be able to show them? Anybody know a gallery space that might be available?"

Like a mother walking cautiously beside her unsteady child on a bicycle, the efficient and considerate Louise led Sarah and Julie in to join the group in the living room. Sarah squeezed onto the large couch beside d.dee, and Julie sat on the floor resting against Sarah's legs. Julie ferociously wished that she had brought something stronger than the Coca-Cola that she was carrying.

"Brenda and I are collaborating on the screenplay, and we have connections in L.A. that are already interested," said Meagan. "I used to date a producer down there when I did a little script consulting. She is pretty well connected."

"Then we've got this almost happening, too," said Brenda. Out of a manila envelope she carefully removed a nine by five of Meagan and passed it around. It was a monochrome long shot view of a toilet stall. Meagan was sitting on the toilet in gym shorts and a muscle shirt. The gym shorts were at her ankles with two dumbbells positioned on either side of her feet. She looked spent and sweaty with a small towel draped around her shoulders and her chin propped in her left hand. She stared directly with a self-satisfied, weary, fuck-you look into the camera.

Brenda explained, "We think the title should be *After Her Workout.*"

"Oh, you look so hot like that," said d.dee obsequiously as she held it lightly on her palms like an open hymnbook. "Your arms!"

Meagan smiled appreciatively at her. "Thanks, d.dee," she said with the little modesty that she could muster. "Well, we aren't afraid of all sides of life, the non-glamorous side, too, the side people would rather hide. No pain; no gain. Our philosophy is to take the bull by the horns no matter how uncomfortable those horns might be. Pooling our connections and different levels of expertise, we're pretty sure that we can find someone interested in marketing this shot. We want to sell it as a postcard in women's bookstores."

"It'll sell out instantly," chirped Brenda. "And while I'm dealing with the bookstores, I can find out what's what because I'm also thinking about writing my autobiography."

Before she could stop herself, Julie asked, "Realistically speaking Brenda, besides friends and relatives, do you think that there will be a market for that?"

A look from Adrienne and a knee from Sarah.

Recovering well was not one of Brenda's strong points. "Well, yes, yes," she stammered, "for . . . for . . . ."

"For the professional woman, to give her motivation and inspiration," finished Meagan. "We're targeting the *professional* woman here, Julie, something you know nothing about." As she spoke, Meagan looked like a lecturer trying to solicit agreement and understanding from the others in the room.

"I'm not trying to minimize your accomplishments or talents," said Julie, continuing to address Brenda, "but you know all about markets.

Without a 'name,' it's extremely difficult for first-time authors. You're first-time, right? Autobiography isn't a common choice for unknowns."

"I have a name. It's Brenda Kinney, for your information."

"I mean a name like, please forgive me, 'Hillary Clinton' or 'Monica Lewinsky.' You're supposed to first write about what you know. Make a name from that. Then you can get people interested in your autobiography from there. They'll remember you were the one who wrote that informative book about whatever. Once you have at least one book under your belt, it will be a far easier sell. No offense, but you're not unique when it comes to successful businesswomen. There is a lot of competition out there."

"Stop being so rude," interjected Meagan as she peered out from behind Adrienne.

"How is that rude?" Julie replied, as she thought how symbolic it was that Meagan was half-hidden. Stand in full view alone for once.

"Criticizing her idea. You're being rude. What do you know about publishing, anyway?"

"I'm not criticizing her idea, Meagan. I am being realistic. I'm trying to help. I read all of this in the manuals when Sarah took that writing course."

Surprisingly, at this point Julie felt no anger. Instead she felt like she had shrunk. Withered and shrunk. There was no way to fight this fight, absolutely no way. The opponent was surly and wrong, but stirred up such convincing diversions that blame exploded all over you for your entire existence. All moves were futile. Meagan had again cleared the path for Cousin Brenda.

Though Meagan always complained about her cousin, Brenda was invaluable to her. Meagan needed to feel constantly superior, and Brenda's cloying insecurity nurtured this. Brenda was weak. Brenda was less attractive. Brenda was easy to manipulate. She was perfect. By always having Brenda around to knock down, Meagan had a guaranteed, foolproof confidence-building system.

"I have also sent some of my poems to k.d. lang that I think she could use in her songs, but haven't heard back yet," said Brenda, who had decided that she was finished with Julie and turned to d.dee for conversation.

"Hey! Me, too!" said d.dee.

A red flag flew up with enormous speed in Julie's mind. A new alliance has been established that will most certainly annihilate her.

"How are you doing, Julie?" Adrienne asked. She was engaged in a delicate juggling act of being conciliatory while simultaneously dishing out reproving looks in all directions.

"I've been well, Adrienne, thanks."

"And you, Sarah?"

"Fine, thanks. Busy."

With faces of stone scorn, Brenda and Meagan kept sending stares emitting as much disgust as possible to Julie. As usual, they were alert and vicious, waiting for something that they could mock or classify as an error in judgment. It was easy to imagine the two of them twenty years ago, thought Julie: plain Brenda scrunched up to precocious Meagan on the school bus seat while they giggled at and taunted the weakest children.

"So, are you still cleaning toilets for a living, Julie, or have you moved on?" asked Meagan.

"Actually, business is really good right now, so I don't do much cleaning anymore. Colleen and I have our hands full with spot checks and management."

"Adrienne tells me that you'd like to have your own little shop someday. What kind of business?" asked Meagan.

"Maybe a used bookstore and CD place, comics, cassettes, maybe."

"Realistically speaking, what kind of market would there be for that and how close are you?"

"Touché, Meagan. Not very close, but there's definitely a market for it." Julie was surprised by her self-restraint. This meekness strategy, rather than unraveling, was very new to her. "I'm still thinking about it. Unfortunately, I can think for a long time. Maybe a sex shop."

"A sex shop!" Meagan looked animatedly at Brenda. They both threw their heads back and laughed a very similar, contrived laugh. "Now, Adrienne didn't mention that."

Adrienne wouldn't be pulled in.

"I think I'd like it because I probably wouldn't get many arrogant customers," Julie explained. "People are pretty docile in that environment usually. I'd like to learn everything and give people advice. I'd like people to feel comfortable instead of shameful. Pleasure is at such a minimum in our lives these days. I want to help provide that, and it's my little way of fighting back against Puritanism. Except there's one big problem."

"What's that?"

"I can't gift wrap. There's going to be a lot of wrapping. A lot of lingerie presents. Big problem."

"I can wrap. I'd work there. I'm an expert wrapper, hey Brenda, Adrienne?" Meagan slapped her cousin's wrist and tickled Adrienne.

"Yeah, she is," agreed Brenda.

"I always wrap for everyone. Let me know if you need any part-time help."

"Do you have retail sales experience?"

"Yup. Footlocker, three years."

"Not squeamish about sexual aids?"

"Who are you talking to, Julie? Are you joking? I'm serious. I'm your woman. Give me a call."

"I'll keep you in mind, Meagan."

Now that the banter was trailing off, Julie decided that it was best that she join the kitchen party. Sounded like they were having more fun in there anyway. "Excuse me, ladies."

* * * *

"You know Kathleen, dark hair, from Ontario? They're fucking now," said Ruth.

"Oh," said Lisa.

"Yeah, yeah," said Naomi, "and Barb and Carmen broke up!"

"Who broke up with whom?" asked Lisa.

"Carmen broke up with Barb," said Ruth.

"That's right," said Naomi. "Honey, you want another beer?" she asked Ruth.

"Sure, hon, thanks."

"How long were they going out again?" asked Lisa.

"About eight years," said Ruth.

"Wow, that's a long time. I thought that they'd stay together forever, grow old together. I thought they were perfect, you know, kind of like inspirational role models for us."

"Nobody's perfect," said Ashley.

"That's right," said Ruth as she turned to Naomi who had come back with two beers. "Things are often a lot different than they look on the outside. You look hard enough and you'll find all the little flaws, isn't that right, sweetie?"

"Right," agreed Naomi.

"Hi, guys," said Julie.

"Hey, buddy," said Lisa as Julie walked into the kitchen and over to where she was leaning against the counter. "How you holding up? You were brave to come. Atta girl, I'm proud of ya. There'd be no parties if all the exes stayed home. Am I right?"

"Thanks, buddy. You're right. Whaddya have to drink? I wasn't going to, so I didn't bring anything but Coke."

"Well, you've come to the right person. I've got beer, beer, beer and vodka."

"I'll take some of that vodka. A double, if you please."

"Screwdriver, okay?"

"Yup."

"Cooooming right up." Lisa poured the vodka and orange juice into a small, transparent, plastic glass and handed it to her. Julie smiled, saluted and raised her glass. "Here's looking at ya, Shriner."

"Cheers."

Julie wiped her mouth with her hand. "Whoa, Harry Heavy Hand! That wasn't a Screwdriver; that was a hammer! Hit me again."

"Certainly, madam."

"A little more. There, that's good." Down the hatch.

Lisa and Julie continued in this manner; pour, salute, drink, smile; pour, salute, drink, smile. The lead in Julie's soul was soon eclipsed by the burning resolve in her gut. Tomorrow she would go on a diet, no more chocolate, well, maybe only on Fridays. She was going to go back to the gym, too, gonna get some new Levis. Who did she think she was talking to anyway?

"Real listically speaking, real listically speakn, bitch, L real listically speakn you."

"Whatcha mumbling about, Julie?" asked her comrade.

Julie held out her glass. "Mmmm, workn my sex shop. Adrn didn't menshun that, mmmm, bich."

Lisa poured another drink and smiled at her friend. "Don't worry 'bout her, buddy. Sheeeez not worth it, really."

"I know whata shoulda said. I shoulda said thaaaaanks Meagan but I'd prefer to haf qualified people workn my shop. Why diddn I think of that?" Julie pounded her knee with her fist. Throat on fire again.

"Youuuuuu'd better slow down a bit," said Lisa and ignored Julie's glass.

Julie stood up straight. "I'm all right."

"Are ya sure?"

"I'm sure, jus pour, please. Sent my poems to k.d. lang. *After Her Workout*, oh right. Connecshuns in LA. I'll show ya connecshuns, like my fist to your face."

"Jules, lettit go. I'm not giving ya anymore if ya keep talking like that."

Julie put one hand on the counter behind her for support and eyed her friend carefully. "Gimme the bottle."

"No."

She licked her lips, tilted her head to the side and considered Lisa further. She sighed. "Gimme the bottle. M'all right."

"Noooo, youuuuu've had nuff, Jules." Lisa pulled the bottle tight against her chest and crossed her arms over it protectively.

"Give me the bottle," she said evenly.

"No."

Point of no return. "Gimme the fucking bottle, you bitch."

"Well, that dozit. Now I'm definitely not givin it to ya."

Julie lunged and grabbed for the bottle. Lisa swerved. Julie hit the fridge. She turned and lunged again, pinning Lisa against the counter. She grabbed her hair with one hand and flailed for the bottle with the other.

"You bish, leggo." Lisa put the bottle on the counter and grabbed Julie's head with both hands and they wrestled about the kitchen. Lisa was smaller, quicker, stronger, and fortunately a kind drunk who knew that Julie didn't fight. She eased Julie down until she was sitting against the kitchen cupboard doors.

"k.d. lang," she slurred. "Snakes, girlfren, drienne. That's it, bish, bish! Megn you come here! Fight lika man with yer arms after your workout!" she screamed. She lurched unsteadily to her feet and grabbed a beer bottle off the counter.

"N who needs you?" she hissed at Lisa as she took a defiant swallow. The defiance lasted less than one second. "Fuuuuuuck!" she yelled as she spit cigarette butts onto the kitchen floor and stumbled into the living room. "School bus, Meaaaaagan."

She flung her fists out and pounded them into Louise's soft arms.

"Honey, honey, Meagan's not here. They left about half an hour ago, Jules. What's wrong? Awwww, it's okay, baby. Don't cry."

* * * *

"Can't you step on it a little, hon? We're gonna miss *Friends*." Meagan leaned over and rubbed Adrienne's knee. They were in Adrienne's white Nissan headed for home; the night was flickering with white headlights, orange turning signals, and red brake lights.

"I'm trying. I don't want to get a ticket or anything, lot of cops out on the weekend. You can see it on Thursday as usual, can't you? The midnight ones are all reruns anyway. God, I hate those brake lights up in the back window. It's not natural to look up there. Who's looking up there? It's like reading subtitles."

"Yeah, but you know my addiction, sweetheart."

Addiction was accurate. Every Thursday night at 8 p.m., Meagan, in anxious anticipation, settled herself in front of the television for her fix, remote on her lap, Corona on the coffee table. (No eating allowed due to possible chewing noise interference.) Meagan sat in a thirty-minute starstruck coma. If you even remotely knew Meagan, then you knew not to disturb her on Thursday evenings between eight and eight-thirty. She was watching *her* show. It had become as much a part of Meagan's lore as the notches on the bedpost. Don't you know not to call Meagan when *Friends* is on? It was a religious ritual.

North Americans have been accused of losing the faith, staying away from their churches, temples, synagogues, and mosques. Overlooked in this observation are the full-to-capacity pews of the mesmerizing, all-powerful religion of television. In manner, humor, and dress Meagan was simply tithing to her favorite television show. They were her thirty sacred minutes of gods. If the phone rang during the show, even during a commercial, Meagan would shake her head in disgust and contempt and let the answering machine pick up. Who was that? Who would dare call here? As soon as the show ended, she'd dash to the phone and call the person back and deliver her emphatically enunciated lecture. "You are *never* to call here at that time again. Never. Do you understand? You don't call a restaurant during lunch hour, do you? No, that's right. And you don't call Meagan when she's watching her show. Is that clear, kids?"

It was another example of Meagan's propensity to manipulate something that had absolutely nothing to do with her to her imagined advantage. She was able to transform what was simply a person sitting on a couch envying the achievements of others into honorable accomplishments of her own. It was irrelevant to Meagan that the wit, craft, and imagination of the people who wrote the show had, with zero effort, been appropriated as her own. She sat down. She pressed a button. But comparable to many a politician, Meagan's image had the invaluable quality of being able to resist reality. She was her own spin-doctor, her own PR firm. She relied on merely watching something to relay that she had taste, that she had class, that she had compatible wit.

"If I were ever desperate enough to write another personal ad," she laughingly told Brenda once, 'MUST LOVE *FRIENDS*' would be the lead."

Despite all the laughs and fantasy it fed Meagan, the sitcom was also responsible for provoking a distressing quandary in her life; namely,

Monica or Rachel? Which one did she love the most? Who was the hottest? Which one should she go for when the chance came? And it would come, just as the Catherine Deneuve dream had prophesied. How could anyone choose between those two?

Adrienne didn't mind listening to Meagan talk about her fantasies of other women. She encouraged it. She found it charming. She enjoyed listening to (rather than sharing) intimate details and found it a fountain of sexual instruction. Pay attention because your partner is writing the manual for you.

I know they'd like me if they met me, too. They are obviously lesbian-friendly with those scripts. I am sure that they'd be attracted to me if they met me at a party. I bet you they know Melissa Etheridge, Ellen. I gotta get to a Melissa Etheridge hot tub party. I'm confident that I'd hit it off with both of them. I just need an opening. Just like with Ashley. "My beautiful Ashley."

"Ashley who? From the party?" Adrienne asked. "Are you daydreaming?"

Meagan panicked for a second and then looked at her reflection in the side-view mirror. "God, I must have been. Sorry, sweetie. Ooooh, as dangerous as talking in your sleep! Judd. Ashley Judd. I haven't told you. I've been holding back, but it's out now. It's one of my most intimate fantasies. I guess you can see a pattern here. I guess it's time." She rubbed Adrienne's inner thigh up and down.

"I'm driving."

"Yeah, me crazy. I can't wait. Fuck *Friends*. Let's get home to bed. Oh, I want you to hear this right now. I want to share it with you, baby. It's going to happen. I can feel it with all my soul. I know that I'm going to meet Ashley Judd someday. It'll be in a hotel, high class of course, maybe in Switzerland. I'm not sure; that part's not clear. The elevator comes up from the parking garage and opens onto the deserted lobby. Deserted, that is, except for me. I get in. It's a wide, thick-carpeted elevator. She's there. It's not hard to read her dismay at the unexpected stop. But as soon as she gets a full view of me, her apprehension and distaste change to warm, sensual approval. Her eyes are piercing. She smiles at me and looks right into the center of my soul. Those eyes that have seen so many beautiful faces smile right at me. Those eyes that have adored so many beautiful bodies are focused on me, and me alone.

Hi, I say shyly. Hi, she says back. The current is unmistakable. You're beautiful. So are you. We can't look away. She wouldn't just call any woman beautiful after all she has seen. Can I interest you in a drink? she says demurely."

"Okay, we're home. Save the rest of it for bed, honey."

Later that night in bed Meagan picked up the thread. "A sex shop?"

"What exactly is your point?" Adrienne leaned over her side of the bed and retrieved her nightie off the floor and slipped it on. She looked at Meagan. "You're beating it to death."

"You mean that you can imagine that loser running a sex shop?" Meagan laughed until she started to cough. "What does she know about that? As much as publishing, I suppose. It also helps if you're at least *a little* bit attractive to work in retail, by the way, especially for a sex shop! It would be nice if the customers were able to imagine the staff having a partner. They want to see someone experienced and desirable. Julie's really not the type, Adrienne. I mean, did you see her hair tonight? What was *that* supposed to be? And that shirt! It was a little loud, wasn't it? I just can't comprehend how someone with incredible style like you could have dated someone with no style for so long."

"She's not a loser, and I find her attractive." Adrienne took her copy of *Cosmo* off the nightstand and tried to ignore Meagan by reading.

"She's a useless human being."

"She has many undeveloped talents. She is also excellent when it comes to business. She could run a successful sex shop."

"Why are you still defending her? Didn't you hear how she called me 'arrogant' tonight?"

"Why are you still attacking her? She didn't call you 'arrogant'. I sleep here, you know, with you."

"I just don't know how you could have stayed with her for so long. And did you hear the way that she was criticizing Brenda tonight?"

"She wasn't criticizing. She was right. Think about it. Who's going to buy Brenda's autobiography?"

For one moment a thought flashed through Adrienne's mind that made her stomach tighten with a heavy ache. It was one of those thoughts you couldn't identify precisely as foreshadowing or anger, because, although it was powerful, it was also mercifully vague and fleeting. If words could have been attached to it they might have been: Is it going to be like this for the rest of our relationship?

"I wouldn't buy Brenda's autobiography; I'd borrow it. And I bet if you weren't her cousin, you wouldn't buy it, either. Anyway, she's going to give you a copy, the copy I borrow. I think Julie was absolutely right."

"What, are you still in love with her or something?"

"I'm not even going to answer that."

Adrienne put the magazine back, reached over and shut off her light. She turned over on her side with her back to her lover. She pulled the sheet tightly around her shoulders, closed her eyes and waited for the theatre to begin.

Meagan could never let things go. Things did not slide off Meagan's back. Some of Meagan's favorite movies were the romantic legends of adventurous knights in which you were guaranteed a scene of a proud, quivering, pretty youth frustrated by the action, or inaction of a beautiful maiden. He was infuriated but linked to her with an inextricable bond that meant no peace. Excruciating desire had to be endured at her tempestuous hands. First he was angry, oh so angry with her, the way that she had wounded him. Then there were harsh words and screaming, maybe it got a little rough, but in the end she was so soft. There was nowhere else for him to go. He would come to her now.

"Do you wish that she were here right now instead of me?"

"Meagan, I told you that I'm not answering that, I'm tired. I'm here because I love you. What I had with Julie is over. I just think that you're too hard on her, that's all, and she too hard on you. It gets exhausting. Good night." Adrienne pulled the sheet even higher so it now covered most of her head.

"What'd she say about me?"

Adrienne lay quiet but unsettled. Only last week at work she had underlined a new passage in her diary. She kept it in the bottom drawer of her desk at work now. She hadn't brought the diary home to Meagan's when she moved in, just something in the back of her mind.

Shut up for once when you touch me. I need you quietly. No bullshit tonight, please. How do you get so fucked up when love is supposed to heal us? Explain to me how you get so lost with something that should raise the both of us up. Try to love me as the person you were before you started recording all the slights against you.

Meagan stared at the ceiling. She stroked her own hair slowly. She was still in charge. There was more than one kind of foreplay. "So, what's she good at again?"

Just touch me.

"I said, what's she good at?" Meagan slid over and put her hand on Adrienne's waist. She wanted to follow the line down. Adrienne burned, but she didn't answer. Meagan kept her hand there for a long time as she kissed the back of Adrienne's neck until she rolled back to her side of the bed, turned off the light and lay with her hands clasped under her head again. Meagan Johnson could wait. She had played this game before. Yes, sir, she could wait, but something that Meagan never thought, though, was that Adrienne could always wait longer.

"I mean, if I don't satisfy you or something, you're free to leave, though you did seem pretty satisfied earlier. You're free to go back. Nobody's stopping you."

The maiden waited and waited and waited until the knight finally moved close behind again, kissing. "No one does it to you like I do," she whispered. "You know that, Adrienne. No one can do this to you except me. Only I know how you like it."

The next day at work Adrienne wrote in her diary: *I've heard desperation a hundred different ways, but I've never felt it. Am I ever going to find someone who can just shut up and lay her hands on me, someone who doesn't think that I need to be mastered?*

Chapter 8 - Lyin' the Tub

Julie awoke fully clothed, lights still on, stereo still on, a cramp like you wouldn't believe in her neck. Vision was a cloudy blur. She tried blinking, but it seemed like her eyes had been glued closed for the night. With a slow, hindered motion like rubbing a lint brush the wrong way, her contact lenses began to unfold back into the proper position. As soon as she could focus relatively clearly, she closed her eyes again and listened to the crackle coming from the stereo speakers. These mornings it was best to keep the eyes closed as long as possible. She was silent and unmoving, which made it seem like her sole body function was breathing. The stench in her mouth was unbearable, however, and she was soon forced out of the chair to the bathroom. Brushing was out of the question with a time bomb for a head, so she squeezed toothpaste directly onto her tongue and put her mouth under the tap for water. She swished and spat.

"Oh, my neck," she said.

She put her hands on either side of the sink and leaned forward close to the mirror. She stared at her face for a long time. She splashed some water on it in hopes of erasing some of the wrinkles and creases. She was absolutely silent because she did not want to speak and be forced to recognize herself. Her mouth tasted like hell, worse than when she had inhaled the Rothmans for the very first time.

The Rothmans were because of Larry's Confectionary. All the elementary school kids used to stop at Larry's on the way home for penny candy. The daytime lady behind the counter at Larry's had deep set, dark, purplish-brown bags under her eyes. They looked like five years' worth of accumulated eye sleep had formed into geological scabs that could be peeled off, but she had neglected to do it. She would morosely count out the coins and then drop the candy into tiny paper bags. As soon as the kids left the store, she'd grab a Rothmans and light it up right behind the counter. She had an ashtray back there. She smoked the cigarette the same plaintive way as she had counted out the candy. While she smoked, she leaned against the back counter and tugged at the ends of her brown-gray hair with her free hand. Thus, the first brand of cigarette that Julie ever tried was Rothmans.

Gripped in anxiety, she quietly pocketed quarters, dimes, and nickels from her brother's coin jar (using both pockets to reduce jangle) and walked guiltily to A&W. She passed the garishly red Hong Kong Palace. She passed the manual car wash where there were guys caressing their damp, dripping cars with soft rags. She cut through the space in the fence and into the drive-in parking lot. The machine was in the lobby. For my mom, she'd say if they asked. She nervously put the coins in and waited for them to drop. Then she pulled the stiff knob at the bottom and the white and blue pack of Rothmans slid out. She grabbed the contraband and stuffed it into the pocket of her yellow spring jacket, scooted out the door and headed for the alley behind the school playground.

"You're such a gimp," Stacy Synder had sneered at her while she was trying to inhale behind the purple sports shack. Stacy was the meanest girl on the playground. She was stocky, two years older, and lived on the far end of the same street. Julie spent considerable time dawdling to stay well behind Stacy on the walks to and from school. "You don't even inhale." But inhaling the Rothmans tasted like hell, just as bad as her mouth did right now.

Julie shuffled back into the living room and tripped on the telephone that was on the floor with the receiver off the cradle. "Shit!" She picked it up and replaced it on top of its stand. Then she rearranged the pillows on the floor, stretched out on them and pulled the afghan over her. Images began to overlap each other; Louise's cozy apartment, Adrienne, Lisa, vodka. Oh, Lisa was gonna be angry. Vodka, Meagan. Lie still, Julie, your headache.

Ring. Transfer interrupted. Was she going to answer it? Ring. Who the fuck called this early on a Sunday morning? Julie shielded her eyes with her hand and tried to focus again. Oh, 12:44, so it wasn't that early, but they should be trained by now. No, wasn't gonna answer. Ring. Who the fuck was disturbing her?

The bastards. Ring. If it went past five rings, she was ripping the fucking thing out of the wall. Ring. Jeeeeeeezus Christ! Have these people no consideration! There, it stopped. Now there's a decent person. After five rings, you gave up. You stopped annoying people who obviously wanted to be left alone on Sunday morning.

Ring. Jeeeeezus Chrrrrrist! Fuckers! That was it!

Julie exploded from her cocoon, rolled across the floor, grabbed the phone cord and pulled the phone down to her. The set crashed onto the floor. Hell to pay.

"What!" she barked into the receiver.

"Julie?"

"Louise?"

"Hi, Julie." In this corner, ladies and gentlemen, we have Julie's debilitating hangover, and in the opposite corner, Louise's considerate, compassionate voice. "I'm very sorry for waking you up, but I thought it would be okay to call. It's 1:00."

"It's 12:47."

"Oh, sorry. How are you? I am just calling to see if you made it home okay."

Shame and regret melt the glaciers of anger with incredible speed.

"Oh, I'm so sorry, Louise. I'm so hung over, you know. Thanks so much for everything last night."

"You made it out of the taxi, okay? We were a little worried about that seeing we had to pour you in."

". . . Taxi?"

"Yeah, the taxi you went home in last night."

". . . Taxi?"

"Yes! We called you a taxi last night. Don't you remember? God, Jules. Sarah had to wrestle you for your car keys; your second wrestling match of the evening, I believe. You wouldn't let anybody go with you though, so that's why I called. I was worried about you."

"I'm fine, just a little hung. Of course I remember the taxi, of course. I'm just a little groggy right now is all; I'm still half asleep."

"Do you need anything, Julie?"

"You're a sweetheart. I'm all right. I just need to go back to sleep and wake up later."

"Okay then, sorry for disturbing you, but I had to check. Talk to you later. Sweet dreams."

Julie wasn't going to have sweet dreams. She had never had a sweet dream in her life. She had bizarre, terrifying, prurient, incomprehensible dreams involuntarily starring the people she was in contact with every day. They were never sweet. "Thanks. I'll call you later. Bye."

"Bye."

Julie hung up the phone and rolled back to her fort. She pulled the afghan back over her head and lay as still as possible. "Taxi, taxi, taxi." This was going to take some time.

Ring, Jeezus. Be nice. It was probably her again.

"Hello."

"Julie, this is Meagan."

"Yeah?" she said, quite bewildered.

"If you fucking call here in the middle of the night again, I will personally come over there and fucking kill you with my bare hands."

"What?"

"I know it was you. Don't you ever fucking do that again! Do you understand? Grow the fuck up."

"I don't know . . . ."

"Adrienne heard you, too. She'd recognize that slobbering anywhere."

"Julie, that's really juvenile," Adrienne's livid voice broke in. "If you threaten us like that again, I am going to call the police."

"Police? Taxi?"

"Don't play dumb, Julie. The threat of arson is very serious. Just when I was thinking that we might have a future as friends, look what you go and do. I'm restraining Meagan from coming over there right now. Get yourself under control, Julie. Get a life!" she screamed and slammed down the phone.

Julie winced and shook her head. She took one of the small pillows and placed it over the receiver on the floor. She got up at six that evening.

* * * *

"It wasn't an accident; she *threw* herself in front of that car," cried d.dee over the phone. "I don't care what anybody says. They don't know. She hadn't been herself for weeks. I just know it was suicide. I just know it!" she wailed.

"Oh, hon, I'm so sorry," said Sarah as she debated whether or not to turn off the pot of macaroni or let it continue to boil. She was so hungry. It was so late, way past dinner.

"They can read things. They know more than we think. They're so much better than damn people. Where will I ever get another cat like Anais?" she sobbed.

"Oh, baby, it's okay. I love you, sweetheart. Hon, you know what? You know what you should do? Right now you should go take a long, hot bath. Right now. Hang up the phone and go boil, I mean, start the water. I know it's hard, but if you do that, baby, you'll feel a little better, and then I'll be there when you get out."

Sarah put the receiver on her shoulder and held it there precariously with her head as she drained the macaroni.

"Why didn't I interpret the signals? I could have prevented it."

Damn lid kept slipping. "Don't blame yourself, hon. You couldn't have known. You couldn't have done anything."

"I felt something in the air that night."

Julie slouched into the kitchen.

"Hi."

"Julie, help me, please," whispered Sarah. "Anais got run over by a car. d.dee thinks it's suicide. Be nice; just talk to her for a few minutes so I can get this done. I'm starving."

"Maybe Anais was trying to free herself from the shackles of matriarchal imprisonment."

"Juuuuulie! Come on, be nice, pleeeeease?" she pleaded.

"Oh, all right."

"Hi, d.dee. It's Julie. Sarah will be right back. Look, I am really sorry about Anais."

"No, you're not," d.dee whimpered. "You don't even like cats."

"I'm a dog person, that's true, but I am starting to like cats more and more as I get older. I used to hate them, but I really liked Anais, truly, d.dee, truly. There was something different about her. She wasn't your usual cat. Remember that time she wouldn't leave my lap? Oh god. Sorry. Don't cry, d.dee. Hold on, here comes Sarah."

Julie opened the fridge and looked for something to drink. She poured herself a large, tantalizing glass of grape juice and sat down in front of the TV to wait for Sarah to finish the call.

"I tell you, I don't remember anything," she said when Sarah got off the phone. "It's a blackout."

"That's stupid, Julie. How could you not remember making the phone call?" asked Sarah between her last ravenous mouthfuls of Kraft Dinner. "Are you sure that you don't want any? This was the last box in your cupboard, too, by the way. You really should eat something."

"It's not stupid. I just don't remember."

"Well, what happens if you do something really dangerous one of these times?"

"I'm not going to do anything dangerous. And do we know for sure that it was even me who called there? It could have been someone else. Meagan has lots of enemies. Or she could be making all this up to attack me."

"I highly doubt it, Julie. But if that's the case, then somehow you have to prove that you didn't do it."

"No, I don't! That's just it! The burden of proof is on them. I don't have to prove that I didn't do it, Sarah. They have to prove that I *did* do it. May I remind you that that's a central tenet of our legal system, ensuring justice for all in this country?"

"I'm not saying the semi-rational Julie who is sitting here right now will do something, but what about the Julie who blacks out? The Julie who fights with Lisa? The Julie who makes 4 a.m. desperate, pathetic phone calls? Can't you just stop at a couple of beers?"

Sarah couldn't possibly know about the other calls, could she? She was talking about only the one to Meagan and Adrienne, right?

There had been a real fucked up one again last month. She had come home good and drunk one night after the breakup and lay on the floor between the stereo speakers for quite some time before deciding to ring her father and thank him for raising her.

A woman's tired, timid voice had answered. "Hello?"

"Who's this?" Julie had bellowed.

"It's Vaneska." She sounded very frightened.

"Vaneska, Vaneska . . . ."

"Yes . . . ."

"Vaneska . . . is my cousin there?" she demanded.

"Who's your cousin, ma'am?"

"Vaneska, everything is going to be okay. I am so sorry, Vaneska. I am so sorry. Go back to sleep, Vaneska."

As Julie tried to suppress Vaneska's small, scared voice, she considered that there were always experiments, like one beer less or a sober Saturday, maybe at the upcoming party. Maybe not. "Are you still coming out this weekend, Sarah?"

"Yup. Look I gotta go. Have to get over to d.dee's ASAP. I know what you're thinking, and the fact is that we're on again, so I don't need any comments from you, thank you very much."

* * * *

Julie and Sarah arrived around eleven. "Fashionably late, Sarah, I tell ya, fashionably late, right in full swing of things."

They didn't know the girl who was having the party, but Sarah knew a friend of hers. It was a warm night, and women were throughout the house and spilling out into the enormous backyard. Outside, most of the women were mingling around the swimming pool, with a few spread out over the lawn all the way to the tall back fence. Julie made her way to the picnic table on the grass at the edge of the pool deck, climbed up and sat down. The house was out near the university campus, so relatively little of Vancouver's artificial light interfered with stargazing in the blue-black summer sky. Julie stared up and tried to remember. Okay, now where was Venus? Over there? Okay, so now where was the Big Dipper? Was that it? Yeah, there was the handle, and there was the ladle. Oh, she was dizzy.

Then so where was . . . ? Where was . . . ? What's-it-called, blood-rushing-to-her-head, oh, she couldn't even remember the name . . . Oh, forget it . . . What about Orion? Anyone could find Orion. Had to find the belt, the sword, the Great Nebula or whatever it was called. Should have paid more attention in class.

A girl with long, brown hair wearing a white tee shirt, no-name jeans, and Birkenstocks weaved her way over to the picnic table, halted and observed Julie for a few moments.

"Are you expecting visitors?" she asked teasingly.

Julie blushed. "No, I'm looking for constellations. Are you any good at that?"

The girl scrambled up beside her. "No, not really. Big Dipper is about all. Hi, I'm Heather," she said and held out her hand.

"Hi, I'm Julie." She shook Heather's hand gently. "Nice to meet you."

"Nice night, isn't it?" said Heather. She put her beer bottle between her legs and untied her ponytail. "Do you know who lives here by the way?"

"No, not really. That little blonde, I think. I came with my friend who knows a friend of hers."

"Me, too. A friend of a friend of a friend thing, but I'm glad I came."

"Me, too."

"You mean you're glad that I came, or you're glad that you came."

"Both."

"So Julie, whaddya do when you're not looking for constellations?"

"I co-own a cleaning company, a maid service, mostly private homes, but a few businesses as well."

"Oh, self-employed. That's good. I hate my job. I'm working as a prep cook at Ricardo's right now."

"You don't like it? That's a good restaurant. I've eaten there."

"Well, I do like cooking, and the people are good, but I'm just not happy there. It's not what I want to be doing. I'd like to have my own restaurant someday."

"What kind of restaurant?"

"I'm thinking kind of a funky, Asian-fusion place."

"Oh. I never know exactly what 'fusion' means, but I'll come there."

Heather smiled gratefully. "Thanks. Are you here with your girlfriend?"

"No, my girlfriend dumped me. She's living with somebody else now."

"Ouch, I'm sorry." Heather took a sip from her beer bottle and held it out to Julie. "Here, have a drink of this. We single gals have to look after one another, ya know?"

"No, thanks. I've got this." Julie smiled impishly and produced a plastic cup from between her ankles on the picnic table bench.

"This beer tastes pret-ty good," insisted Heather.

"Okay, twist my arm," said Julie. Heather passed her the bottle, and she took a drink.

"Women, hey," said Heather. "Can't live with 'em; can't live without 'em."

"That's for sure."

"So, if you could be a fly on the wall of anyone in history, whose wall would you be on?" Heather asked.

"Am I a polyglot fly?"

"What's a polywhat?"

"Glot, polyglot. It's someone who speaks many languages."

"There's no such word as polywhatever," giggled Heather. "I've never heard of that."

"Just because you've never heard of it. Look it up."

Heather grinned at her, half-persuaded. "I will look it up as soon as I get home. In fact, I feel like looking it up right now. There must be a dictionary in the house."

"Oh, just trust me. You trust me, don't you?"

"Yeah. All right you're a polywhatever fly."

"Okay, then, in Hitler's office. You see, I would have to understand German."

"Ooooh, that's morbid."

"What about you?"

"Cleopatra's wall."

Heather leaned over and lasered her pleading eyes deep into Julie's. She wobbled even closer. "Do you think I'm pretty?"

"Yeah," Julie lied. Not my type, she thought, but not so bad. Her smile was kind of nice. Julie kept the bottle and took another drink. Her eyes were kind of nice, too. What were they brown? Hazel?

"Hold on," said Heather. "I'm gonna get some more beer. Don't move! I'll be right back."

"Grab me one, too!" Julie yelled after her.

Heather scurried over to the house and charged in the back door. Less than two minutes later she re-emerged, jogged back over to the picnic table and climbed eagerly up beside Julie again. Like a game show hostess, she pulled two chilled bottles of beer from behind her back and displayed them.

"Ta-daaaaaaaa, right or left?"

"Right." Julie playfully grabbed the beer from her hand before Heather had a chance to give it to her. She wiped the bottle on her jeans and twisted off the cap.

"Here's looking at ya, Shriner."

"Hey, my dad was a Shriner. Cheers."

"Did he drive the little cars?"

"Yup. Weird, hey?"

"No kidding."

She did have a nice smile.

There was a transformation occurring. It would have been astounding had it happened suddenly in the daylight, but because it happened alcohol-aided, slowly and subtly on a sweet summer night when you could sit outside on a picnic table in your tee shirt showing off your tan, it materialized rather inconspicuously. Heather became very pretty . . . and incredibly sexy. Julie began to contemplate things that she'd only seen in videos.

They chatted pleasantly and laughed and flirted and teased, during which time Heather scooted back into the house many more times. Not too long after her most recent trip, they began kissing uninhibitedly on the picnic table. After a rather lengthy session, they pulled apart, looked shyly at each other and took drinks from their beers.

"Wow," said Heather. She didn't look at Julie, who was concentrating solely on the beer bottle between her feet. "That was nice."

"Yeah," agreed Julie.

What was there to say in those awkward moments after the attraction has been acknowledged, after the regular boundaries have been invaded? Did you talk about it? Were you practical and said, "Look, I'm really attracted, but I'm having my period and . . . ." Prudent? "Okay, it's really important that we practice safe sex." Truthful? "It's been a long time and the intimacy terrifies me, but I really want to know you." How exactly did you say that you wanted to end unsatisfying, inhibited sex and talk candidly to your partner without shame, in hopes of achieving maximum mutual pleasure? And especially, what did you do if you were not alone where you could nudge each other in the direction of the bed and progress Hollywood-style, but were on a picnic table in the middle of a backyard during a raucous summer party? One way was to continue drinking anything that you could get your paws on until your inhibitions were so entirely numbed that process didn't matter anymore. The first suggestion won. That was it. Simple, really.

"I know a place," said Heather, and she took Julie's hand and tugged her down off the picnic table. Julie followed obediently.

They staggered over the lawn and through the back door. Heather stopped in front of the fridge. "Wait a sec." She opened the door, knelt down and pulled open the crisper. She rummaged under a large floppy head of red leaf lettuce and triumphantly pulled out two more bottles of beer. She held them in one hand, grabbed for Julie's with the other and led her to the basement stairs. "I saw a spare bedroom down here."

They descended the stairs tipsily. Heather led Julie past a group of women around the pool table. "Hi, guys," said Heather with a giggle.

"Hi," one of them answered sluggishly. The others merely nodded and looked extremely uninterested in the new visitors.

She led Julie past a netless ping pong table to a closed door in the far corner. "A real rec room," mumbled Julie. Heather opened the door and fumbled for the light.

"Fuck off!" yelled a woman's voice from the darkness. "Get outta here! Leave the light off!"

"Aw shit," said Heather and closed the door. "Sorry, ladies." She turned and looked apologetically at Julie. "Oops, occupied," she said and started to laugh. "Damn it. No sign. No lock." She set her beer on the ping pong table and Julie did the same. They began necking again. Over Heather's shoulder, between breaths, Julie was trying to read the "Drunk Clock" above the wet bar. Was it eleven-twenty or eleven-forty? Cinderella had to know.

"I can't wait," mumbled Julie.

"Me, neither. Let me think. C'mon." Heather grabbed the beers and Julie's hand once again and led her back to the bathroom near the bottom of the stairs. "No one's in here. They can use the upstairs one," she whispered. "C'mon."

There was a very familiar vague reluctance tapping at Julie's brain, but like so many times before she ignored it and instead said, "K."

Heather put the lid down and sat on the toilet seat, and Julie sat on the edge of the tub.

"Well, let's have a little refreshment after our loooong journey," proposed Heather. "Cheers, Shriner." They clinked bottles and drank. Heather leaned over and began to kiss, lick, and suck Julie's neck. Julie kept drinking her beer. No rush. Heather put her hand under Julie's shirt and ran it up her back.

"Mmmmmm, you're so soft." She lifted Julie's shirt up and began to kiss all over her back. Julie took another drink. Heather reached around and took the bottle from Julie's hand and set it in the tub. She stood up and pulled Julie to her feet. She pushed her gently against the towel rack and they kissed and kissed and kissed and ran their hands all over each other. Heather dropped her right hand down to aid her left that had been unsuccessfully trying to unbutton the top button on Julie's Levis.

Julie put her arms tightly around Heather's neck and kissed her hard. This was the signal telling Heather that Julie was willing to participate in anything, absolutely anything at that moment provided Heather took charge like was expected of any good lieutenant. Heather, however, continued to fumble and fumble with the button until finally Julie impatiently interrupted, with "Here let me," and reached down and undid it herself. Heather unzipped the zipper and tried to reach two fingers in, but the jeans were too snug.

"Hold on," Julie said, and she began to slide her jeans down herself. Soon they were at her ankles and she and Heather were once again kissing desperately. Heather tiptoed her fingers through the front of Julie's new, white Calvin Klein boxers (that's why the jeans were so tight) and began stroking her as Julie moved against her.

"Oh, that feels so good," Julie whispered into Heather's neck.

"You want more dontcha?" whispered Heather.

Julie brushed the hair away from Heather's ear and began to bite it.

"Hellloooo! What are you doing in there?" someone pounded on the door.

"Fuck!" said Heather.

"Hurry up! You've been in there forever! There are people waiting! Come on!"

"Fuck!" said Julie.

"Just ignore 'em," said Heather as she pushed her fingers deeper. "Oh, you're so wet. Does it feel good?"

"Come on! Get outta there!"

"Shit!" said Heather.

"Shit!" said Julie.

"We gotta let 'em in," said Julie. "Mood's ruined. Be right theeeeeeere!"

"Yer right," agreed Heather. "They'll break down the door, those dykes. We gotta let 'em in. But I can't leave you, not now. I know! Lyin' the tub."

"What?" Julie whispered back.

"Lyin' the tub. That way ya don't hafta put your jeans on."

"Noooooo, I don't know."

Heather pulled the shower curtain back all the way and held it chivalrously for Julie. Julie didn't move. Heather put her hands on Julie's shoulders and shook them firmly. "Just trust me. Remember, I trusted you." She nodded and stared directly into her comrade's eyes as seriously as if they were vowing a death pact. "Lyin' the tub n we can wait till they leaf." She picked up Julie's bra and threw it into the tub.

"Heeeeeeey!" protested Julie.

"Don't worry, s'not wet. Now get in, and I'll get on top of ya after I unlock the door. Hurry!"

Someone hammered the door again.

"K," said Julie and got in.

"Cooooominnnnnng," crooned Heather.

"Ouch, Jeezus!" said Julie.

She pulled the beer bottle from under her and set it up in the corner with the drugstore conditioner and shampoos. She lay still and soggy on her back in the green enamel tub and closed her eyes. Heather quietly unlocked the door, tiptoed back and clambered in, not entirely gracefully, and lay on top of Julie and pulled the shower curtain closed. "Okaaaaaay, you can come innnnnnn now."

The door flung open and a woman's voice said, "What the fuck are you doing in here?"

"S'okay, just go about your business, and don't mind us, okay?" said Heather.

"Whatever," said the voice. "I've gotta piss like a racehorse."

Heather smoothed the hair out of Julie's eyes and kissed her. Julie put her arms around Heather's waist and held tight. They stayed that way for about five voices. That's when Julie said, "Uumm, Heather, not that I'm not enjoying myself or you're heavy or anything, but lying here is sorta making me upset to my stomach."

* * * *

"And so you just threw up all over her?" asked Sarah.

"I don't know if I'd say it was necessarily *all* over her," answered Julie.

"Well, if she was lying on top of you and you were necking then it probably was all over her."

"How would you know? Were you there?"

"Maybe I was. How would you know with the shower curtain closed? Little ducks on it, right? That must have tasted nice for Heather."

"Shut up. Don't talk like that. It doesn't become you."

Sarah grinned widely at Julie. "Anyway, I think that she'd be really sweet sober. She's cute. Are you going to see her again? I think you should."

"Don't know."

"What do you mean, 'don't know?' Here's a chance for you to forget all about Adrienne. Someone who is obviously interested in you, and you want to ignore her and continue to mope around. You should call her or at least let me fix something up with Debbie. Come on. You said that you'd be interested."

"I'm not moping. It's not called moping. For your information, it's called devastation. I don't want to forget about Adrienne. Don't you understand?"

"I do understand, Julie, but you have to face reality at some time. Adrienne's with Meagan. Period. She's not coming back."

"It's not period. It's never period. It was period with Adrienne and me, too. And Meagan's not reality. What's reality? You're hardly an expert on reality. I'm not attracted to Heather."

"You were attracted on the picnic table . . . in the bathtub."

"Okay, let me rephrase that. Without alcohol, I am not attracted to Heather. She's not my type. There's no passion."

"You're too picky."

"You're not picky enough."

"For the sake of our friendship, I'm going to ignore that, Julie."

"Sorry. I can't help it, but Heather-hates-her-job just doesn't do anything for me. God, I've got a splitting headache."

"Not everyone can be as gorgeous as Adrienne, you know."

"I know and that's why I'm cursed."

"You're not cursed. Can't you just love someone for what's inside? For inner beauty? Are you that shallow?"

"Yes."

"Are you serious?"

"I don't know. I guess so. I try to not be, but it's hard."

"What about the inside, Julie? I mean really, take a hard look. d.dee says . . . ."

"d.dee has to say it."

"What does that mean?"

"Nothing."

"No, what does that mean?"

"I mean that you use what you have, and if you don't have it, then you have to console yourself in a different way."

"Are you calling my girlfriend ugly?"

"I didn't say that."

"It's what you implied."

"That's not what I said. You're putting words in my mouth. Not ugly, she just doesn't do anything for me. It's like Heather; it's my personal opinion only. I can't speak for the rest of the world."

"Why? You do the rest of the time."

"Sarah, let's not go there."

"We're already there."

"Okay, I don't find d.dee physically attractive, personal opinion only. And to me her politics are like a hideous accessory. I am sorry. I know I shouldn't be like that, but I am. I know the Adriennes in the world get most of the chances. I know. They get a million, and Heather's lucky if she gets one good one. I'm not saying that it's right, but that's how it is. I don't get very many chances, either, and that's why I'm desperate to get Adrienne back. I'm ashamed to say it, but there it is. Now you know. I had it. I lost it. I can't lose it, Sarah. I had it in my hands. I can't let it slip through."

"Well, d.dee doesn't find you attractive, either."

"She said that?"

"Personal opinion only."

"She said that? When did she say that? What'd she say?"

"Why don't you ask her the next time you see her? By the way, are you coming over there with me? I have to water her plants."

"Good thing you're not separated anymore."

"Even if we were, I would still be doing it. This is something we agreed upon a long time ago. She's away at a conference, and they need to be watered. Simple. And I am getting really tired of you continually bringing this up. It's old hat, Julie."

"Why can't she get someone else to water them? Oh, forget it. I already know the answer. Yeah, I'll come, and let's get something to eat after."

"Okay."

* * * *

It was in the Bible what d.dee was doing a coast away. As Julie and Sarah were speaking, d.dee was committing number seven--adultery in the heart. That was a terribly inadequate description for it really, for it wasn't just her heart; it was between her legs and in her hands, in her nerve endings, and on her scalp, and deep inside her stomach. At the precise moment that Sarah, her trusting and faithful girlfriend, was forming in her larynx the words that were milliseconds away from being released by her vocal cords, d.dee was sitting in an organic restaurant overwhelmed with a powerfully renewed, weak-kneed devotion for another woman. That exact second as words about watering were leaving a loyal Sarah's lips, d.dee was sitting across from Jacqueline Mackenzie-Gould in a state of respectful reverence and simmering lust.

"And I hope that in this, my latest book, I am able to convey the ethos adequately. Of course," and Mackenzie-Gould paused here to laugh self-deprecatingly, "it might just be a pyrrhic victory because my husband says 'Who are you?' when I walk through the door at night." She shook her head from side to side as she tapped her water glass with candy apple-red fingernails.

Swooning. Wasn't that what Elvis used to make the girls do? Wasn't that the dominant adjective used to describe the hysterical mob of teenagers as they rushed the Beatles? Tears and fainting fits, a legion of d.dee's with hankies. There's a certain kind of woman that makes women who love women say: "Why, oh why, oh why couldn't this woman be a lesbian?" She's perfect! It's too cruel, too cruel, thought d.dee.

As an activist, d.dee had acquired numerous membership acronyms, like GLAM (Gay/Lesbian Anarchist Movement) and LASS (Lesbians Against Social Structures). This conference, however, was a WEAL

(Women in Education Advising Language) conference. And though she did occasionally show up at the other ones, absolutely every WEAL conference was attended by the incredibly gorgeous, lesbian-baiting, but straight, Dr. Jacqueline Mackenzie-Gould; author of four books, Professor of Women's Studies, advisor to numerous political and educational councils, and one of the most gay-friendly women on God's Green Earth.

It was a crushing (but forgivable) insult to d.dee and her friends that Dr. Mackenzie-Gould was married to the antithesis of all that a woman like that was supposed to stand for, a man. Every characteristic flooded in entangling nuances said that she should have been a lesbian. She was, after all, constantly surrounded. Most of her confidantes, peers, pawns, students, and devotees were all on the team. Never was there any revulsion from her, no inherent misgiving detected, only reassurance, acceptance, and understanding. Then, what circuit had misfired?

What was the one malfunction that derailed an otherwise perfect specimen?

"Quite simply, my dear, cock." That's how Dr. J had explained it to a trembling, intoxicated d.dee who had showed up at her room carrying a bottle of champagne, two glasses, a rose, and three years worth of swollen expectations. "I am sorry, d.dee. I love women. You know that. I love you, too. I really do, but I love cock too much." Poor d.dee, undone by seamed nylons and semantics, black lipstick and erudition. Dr. J did indeed know where to find a captive audience.

For three years since meeting Mackenzie-Gould, d.dee had attended every conference, every meeting, every book signing, every function possible just so she could be near her. This time they were at an out-of-town convention. d.dee had waited for this chance with remarkable, uncharacteristic patience. This particular conference was at a Toronto hotel, and it was also one of the only ones with no male convention delegates. That was why d.dee felt bold and optimistic. The key was, she believed, to whisk Dr. J away from her daily routine and get her into more relaxing surroundings, especially away from any male influence. According to the majority of seduction articles of which d.dee was a diligent student, borderline cases required such an environment. Once you got her away from her demanding regular pursuits, you employed a universal, some might say rather primitive tactic; you got her drunk. Everyone knew that those Ladies' Nights at the bars weren't really *Ladies'* Nights. They were *Men's* Nights. I present you with a bar full of drunken women. You're very welcome.

On paper it was flawless; in d.dee's mind it was beautiful; in practice it was futile. It was a delayed futility though, revealed only after the door of room 918 opened and exposed her frail plan. Dr. J led d.dee to the bed but instead of swooning into her arms with desire, she had gently sat her on the edge and held her hand while she explained why she could not be a lesbian for her. In thesis style, she tenderly laid out the reasons why she could not reciprocate d.dee's love. It was not because she didn't have a love of women, but because her love of man prevented her from living that unexplored life. Her husband was gentle and caring and sensitive, like a woman. She loved him. He was her soul mate, and she couldn't imagine life without him. She stroked d.dee's hands and her hair. They hugged while they both cried. Then they wiped the tears away and drank some champagne.

"No use wasting this," said Dr. J, and the mood brightened as they laughed, discussed a little Derrida, and eventually kissed goodnight on the lips.

So compassionate had Dr. J been, so human and warm and magnanimous and honest, that d.dee awoke the following morning even more in love. And although it was painful for her to accept the gentle, polished rejection and reasons why, she now had fresh, new, vibrant tape to play. She ran it over and over in her head like space shuttle footage. There. See it again. Pause. She puts her hand on my knee, and then she reaches up and strokes my cheek. Now watch. Here her arms come around my neck. Look how she pulls me to her. She kisses me right on the lips. Freeze it there. Play it again in slow motion. Play it again, her lips against mine. Play it again. There she is sitting next to me in her black teddy, weeping.

This private encounter was quite enough to temporarily satisfy d.dee's yearning. It was between her and Dr. Mackenzie-Gould, something that was uniquely theirs. No one could intrude. No one could distract Dr. J, and no one could take it away from d.dee. This was what d.dee was replaying and narrating as Sarah was dutifully climbing the stairs to water her girlfriend's plants.

* * * *

d.dee's don't-you-dare-say-bachelor apartment was in a quiet, old, tree-sheltered brick building downtown. It had heavy wooden front doors and thick carpets that muffled the wide hallways into a still serenity. There was no elevator in the building, so Julie and Sarah climbed the four long flights to d.dee's floor.

Next time I am counting these steps, Julie thought: They're so thick. They're like two in one.

Sarah unlocked the door, and they entered d.dee's home, her attempt at a starving artist ambience. It was below the poverty line all right, but it was poverty devoid of genuine artistic traces. It was an inauthentic assembly that came off looking like a tired and mediocre little room with nothing being sacrificed for art. Posters announcing events were tacked up unevenly about the walls: a brash lesbian comedienne, a magnetic feminist performance artist, an inspiring San Francisco-based impromptu troupe, erotic dyke photography exhibitions, devilish, women's nights and grave poetry readings. Over her bed in the corner of the room, ripped from magazines, were pictures of Jodie Foster, Ani DiFranco, Gillian Anderson, and Marilyn Monroe. The badly scratched, dull, hardwood floor was covered with a navy, gold, and white imitation Persian rug. d.dee kept saying that she was going to refinish the floor some day, but she never seemed to get around to it. A slant of crusty paperbacks and an assortment of textbooks inhabited a board and brick bookcase. The thickest among the textbooks was a prominently placed edition of Foucault's *Ethics, Subjectivity, and Truth.* There was also a pile of about thirty dog-eared issues of *Girlfriends* magazines. However, you'd only ever hear d.dee declare that she had been "influenced by Foucault," never something like, "I've been influenced by *Girlfriends.*"

Julie knelt down and spent a few minutes flipping through a shabby copy of *Nightwood* and some slight volumes of poetry. d.dee read women poets only, no men.

"'Romantic,' they call that 'romantic'? You know what your Lords Byron and Shelley were up to, don't you? And it wasn't sitting on the porch making up ghost stories."

Julie stood up and went and sat on the small, brown sofa. She sunk down into the worn cushions as they ejected a helping of crumbs into her lap. There was a thick coloring book on the coffee table. Julie picked it up and opened it. The conspicuous absence of any wild scrawl outside the lines clearly showed that this book did not belong to a child. It belonged to someone who liked to pretend that she was still like a child. There was no blue hair. There were no orange shoes or purple coconuts. There were no gigantic, diagonal, dyslexic-looking signatures in block letters. While Julie could never understand why, she knew exactly what. Among the main images that d.dee strived to construct, was one that she had remained "childlike." She didn't have to grow up; she could live in Never Never Land forever. She wanted people to speak of her innocence; the trusting, naive, fragile d.dee versus a demoralizing, harsh, unforgiving world. That a lack of innocence may not be such an undesirable state never entered the dialogue.

d.dee desired to be untainted with a revolving innocence that she could lose and then gain again at will. At thirty-two years of age, she giggled and snuggled up to Sarah in bed and asked for green icing and pink sparkler candles on her birthday cake. She bought a 48-pack of crayons and *Betty and Veronica* comic books. She was d.dee, who carried a plastic lunch bucket with *Star Wars* characters on it. d.dee, who bought Sesame Street Bubble Bath and sang in the tub, "one of these things is not like the other . . . ." d.dee, who begged Sarah to take her to the amusement park, and no matter if it was the Tea Cups or The Octopus, or even the dreaded Sky Diver, she clutched half-frightened, half-euphoric to her girlfriend's arm and squealed for the duration of the ride. Then, recovering quickly from her terror and convinced that she was irresistibly cute, d.dee would flounce along with pink candy floss and plead with Sarah to knock down milk bottles with a baseball or burst a balloon with a dart in order to win a stuffed toy. Her bed was covered with them (purchased, since Sarah sucked). There were adorable elephants, friendly pigs, cute frogs, gentle bears, and domestic mice, even a few Snoopys and a Raggedy Ann.

It took Sarah a long time to convince d.dee that the bed wasn't big enough for the twenty or so of them. Even when she had accomplished that, every night d.dee had to place them gently and tenderly, in order, on the floor at the foot of the bed and cover them with a blanket. Initially, Sarah helped willingly with this cute task, but it soon became a chore and, after the Mr. Mulligan blowout, she absolutely refused to help ever again. "He doesn't go there, Sarah. He goes next to Mr. Wiggles!"

If I were alone, what treasure I could find, Julie thought. "It's weird being in someone's place when they're not here," she said.

"Yeah, even for me," replied Sarah.

"Maybe it's because it's a glimpse of what it would be like if d.dee, god forbid, never came back," said Julie. She put the coloring book down and reached over and picked up the television remote control.

"Julie, you don't have to watch television. We're only going to be here a couple of minutes."

"Just want to see what's on. I'm bored."

"I'd rather you didn't."

"Why not? I just wanna see what's on."

"Look, Julie, d.dee doesn't like people to watch television when she's not here."

"Like she's gonna know."

"Julie, could you just respect her wishes, please?"

"Jeezus Christ, there's that *respect* word again. This has nothing to do with *respect!* It's always respect this and respect that from you two, a total misuse of the word. Can't even argue against it just because it sounds right. What is the harm in watching a little television? How can I possibly be offending anyone?"

"It's not me, Julie. It's d.dee. She's particularly sensitive about it."

"She's particularly sensitive about everything."

Sarah picked up a note off the kitchen counter and brought it over to Julie. "Okay, read this."

"The most common cause of household fire is from leaving the television set on," read Julie. "Avoid turning the set on and thereby avoid the chance of a mishap."

"You know, Sarah, I am sorry, but your girlfriend is a mishap, an emotional mishap. And what if it's contagious?"

"You're the one with emotional problems, Julie."

"Yeah, you're my best friend."

Chapter 9 - Make No Mistake

Adrienne, can you please meet me tonight at Lavender's at seven? I just want to talk to you and explain what happened. I won't keep you long. I swear to god, I don't remember making that call. I can't call your place because Meagan will kill me, and I don't want to bother you at work. Please, just a few minutes. I'll explain everything and then you never have to see me again if you don't want to, I promise. Julie.

"How does that sound, Sarah?"

"Well, it's better than the first one, that 'I wasn't going to tell you, but now I've been forced to: Adrienne, I have only six months to live' crap."

"Desperate times call for desperate measures. And these are desperate times. Anyway, how does it sound?"

"It sounds okay, but it's highly unlikely that she will meet you. She's probably still really pissed off at you, Julie. You should just call her at work and then you'd know immediately instead of going through all this."

"You know that I can't stand direct rejection, and she could be with a client or in the middle of something and not be able to answer freely. This way, if she doesn't show up, then it's indirect rejection, much easier to handle."

"You've become somewhat of an expert on this, haven't you?"

"They're called 'defense mechanisms,' Sarah. But you know what I've been thinking? You know what could be a big part of all this?"

"No."

"That it has been too *painful* for Adrienne to call. What could she say in the mall? It was too uncomfortable to talk, no privacy whatsoever. Now we've got that first time over with and out of the way. She still wants to say a lot of things to me, but how can she? She's being watched all the time. She probably has a lot of regrets but is being so controlled by Meagan that she doesn't even realize it. And now I've done the stupid drunk thing and just compounded matters. Yes, she was angry, but she knows it was a stupid drunk thing. She lived with me. I know her livid. It wears off quickly. That's why I have to leave her this note and arrange to meet her without Meagan knowing and without putting her on the spot at work. Last time, see, Meagan knew, you see."

Sarah only stared at her friend.

"And it's Thursday," Julie continued. "If her schedule is similar to before, then Meagan's home watching *Friends,* so she can spare a few minutes."

"I don't know, Julie. I'm not saying anything to encourage you. Why don't you just give Heather a chance since she keeps calling?"

"Yeah, I know, you'd prefer to discourage me. Well, I have to do it, Sarah. You have to take risks, chances in this life or it's not worth living, am I right?"

Sarah only stared at her friend.

* * * *

Julie approached Adrienne's white Nissan as nonchalantly as possible. Why the paranoia? She wasn't doing anything illegal. It was certainly not illegal to put a note on a friend's car. It could be a flyer for all anyone knows. Maybe if she held it like a flyer. Chuck's words about customs inspectors being able to spot people "acting strangely" a mile away were suddenly amplified in Julie's brain. Chuck had said that when she used to work at the airport that it was only the slightest, almost undetectable (to the untrained eye, that was) thing that gave people away. She said it became your sixth sense. It could be something like only the ill-timed avoidance of eye contact or a revealing body posture.

"We found a monkey in a suitcase once, drugged, from Mexico. We had to put it down. We had no other choice. At least it never had to wake up. And one time, I felt bad about this one, there was a lady acting really strangely, and it turned out that she had cancer and was completely bald and was wearing this long, black wig. It was just the wig that set her off. And then of course, you have the liars, the ordinary run-of-the-mill liars, so many liars. 'Do you have any mangos in your suitcase, ma'am?' 'No.' 'Are you sure?' 'Yes.' 'You're absolutely sure that you don't have any mangos in your suitcase?' 'Mmmmm, no mangos.' 'Open the suitcase, please ma'am'. Wham, full of mangos."

Julie looked guiltily in both directions and slipped the note under the windshield wiper. All the way home she felt that someone was just about to tap her on the shoulder and hand it back to her with admonishment.

She arrived at Lavender's at 6:40 with her stomach as tight as plastic wrap stretched across a dish. During those minutes of dense emotion, Julie marveled at what motivated her to crawl out of bed every day. How had she moved during the last several months? How had she moved before she met her?

The very instant that she arrived, as soon as she walked through the door, Julie knew resolutely that Adrienne was not coming, but she pushed it down. She had to rouse some optimism for a short time at least or it would be too unbearable. She ordered an iced cafe latte. That passed a few minutes. It was 6:45 and she could have been panicking for nothing. Who knew anyway? Anticipation leapt cautiously within her. She could be on her way right now, looking for a parking space. Feelings: disembodied, out of control, jumbled and contradictory. It was 6:55--take deep breaths now. She wasn't coming. She wasn't coming. She knew it when she wrote the note. Why did she have to write it anyway? Couldn't she just have left things alone? Now here she was waiting again. That was the worst. Why did she have to open it up again? She was so stupid!

Seven o'clock--she wasn't there, but mathematically the possibility still existed because there were sixty seconds to 7:01; sixty more chances for Adrienne to appear at the appointed hour. Don't forget that. She could walk through that door during any one of those seconds, and we hadn't even factored into the equation yet that her watch might be slow. Realistically, we could be counting seven o'clock for three or four minutes. Even five.

What did the clock say here? One minute to, see? Now, now, NOW! She could be parking the car, walking down the sidewalk and just about to push open the door. Julie looked over at the entrance. NOW!

It was 7:12 and some clarity slowly began to seep back in, but she knew that it was better not to leave just yet. Julie had taught herself not only to ease into the exquisite things, but also into the painful ones. You couldn't just jump up and carry it fresh and virulent like it was. Don't take it all with you. Let some of it evaporate here. She couldn't take it all home again anyway. She just couldn't take it there alone right now. This was absolutely the last time that she got her stupid hopes up. She meant it. Sarah was right, move on. Move on! Don't just say it, DO IT! Believe it! Have some convictions for once. Stand firm. Fuck her if she didn't want her. There were plenty of other fish in the sea, plenty. Work out a little bit, get some new clothes, and venture back into the dating circuit. Take your dating destiny into your own hands, ladies. There were times that Adrienne could look repulsive anyway. Hell, give that Heather a call, or let Sarah fix something up with Debbie. If Adrienne wanted to waste her life with that dog Meagan, then let her. It was her loss, her severe loss. She'd be sorry one day when she realized the horrendous mistake that she had made, and she would realize it. *Make no mistake about that.* That was it, from this moment on, nothing, absolutely nothing! No calls, no mail, no thoughts; she was erased completely. She was totally, one hundred percent deleted and annihilated from Julie's life.

But maybe there was a message at home.

Julie ran like she hadn't run since elementary school track meet days. She flew into her apartment right at the answering machine. Merciful lord Jezus Christ in heaven the red light was flashing! She jammed the play button with her finger and waited tensely. "Hi, Julie. It's Adrienne. I'm sorry I couldn't make it tonight. You didn't give me enough warning, and I had other plans. I'm still furious with you, but you are right, we have to clear everything up once and for all. I'll call you in a few days. I just wanted to tell you that I got your note and I'm not ignoring you, because I know how you panic. Bye."

She grabbed the receiver.

"Sarah, Sarah, listen to this! Hold on, I have to rewind it." She impatiently held the receiver over the answering machine and played back the message for Sarah. "Did you hear that? 'Because I know how you panic?' See? She still cares about me, Sarah! If she didn't love me, if I meant nothing, she wouldn't be concerned about me panicking, would she? That would be the least of her worries. Am I right? Am I right? What do you think?"

"Julie, I really can't say. I'd have to hear it again."

"Okay, I'll play it for you again, hold on. Now listen this time...Okay, could you hear it better?"

"A little, but not much. I don't know, Julie. She sounded the same to me. You know her better than I do, though. Yes, it's a good sign that she called, but you never know with women. You never know what they're thinking. Maybe all she means is exactly what she said."

"But she said that she was 'sorry,' Sarah. And that means that she's still very much concerned with my feelings. She wouldn't be concerned if she didn't care. And she didn't want me to think that she was ignoring me. If she hated me and wanted to get back at me, she'd let me go crazy. And she said that she'd call later; she wouldn't say that if she didn't mean it; I know Adrienne. If she just wanted to forget the whole thing, then she wouldn't have said anything. But I really think the key is the panic thing. She could have tortured me, but she didn't. She could have just ignored me, but she didn't. Instead she was compassionate, and you're usually not compassionate with your ex-lovers so soon--especially after the other night. You see what I mean?"

"Yeah, I see what you mean. Hey, are you still coming out tomorrow night?"

"That's still on?"

"Of course. I think it will be really good for you to get back into the scene."

"You mean the dating scene?"

"Sort of."

"I'm not into the dating scene."

"I mean the 'go-out-and-have-a-couple-of-drinks-and-look-at-some-women' scene, the potential dating scene. It doesn't have to be actual. Potential, Julie, potential."

"Who is going to be there again?"

"Me, of course, and d.dee and some of her friends from the Crisis Center. I don't know exactly yet. The plan is to meet at d.dee's first for a potluck and watch some of the Olympics and then go after that."

"Hate potlucks, never know what to bring. Hate potlucks."

"You can bring dessert like you always do. You know you don't have to cook. Buy some ice cream or pick up some cake or fruit."

"Sure, whatever you say, Sarah. I'm in, baby. Life is good." Julie hung up the phone and danced into the kitchen.

Chapter 10 - She's Your Cousin, Then?

Julie counted aloud as she went. "Nine, not counting the landing. That's two in one, so that's eighteen steps times four is seventy-two. Seventy-two more reasons for Adrienne to love my new ass. She will notice the difference, too! And how often do you come here, or how often did you used to come here?" she said as she puffed up the last couple steps.

"Forget about it, Julie." Sarah knocked, and they went in. "Hi, we're here."

"Come on in," said d.dee. "We're just finishing up here, so give us a second."

"Sure."

"Personally I'm sick of the pseudo-generics," d.dee continued. "If I hear 'coed' one more time, I'm gonna scream!"

"Oh, me too," agreed a girl sitting on the floor.

"Okay then, let's wrap things up," said d.dee. "As caucus leader of GLAM, I propose the motion that we initiate our investigation into the heterosexist bias in late 19th and early 20th century fairy tales and report back here with our findings in three months. All in favor, unanimous? Good, that's it, then. We're adjourned."

"Oh, wait d.dee. One more thing," said the girl on the floor.

"Yeah, what's that, eleven?"

"GLAM has to decide our position on the Rikki Fines affair. Are we going to pledge our support for her fight for the right to keep first prize in the Win a Date with Britney Spears contest?"

"Oh right, right. I forgot about that," said d.dee. "Thanks for reminding me, eleven. Full support. Take care of that for us, please."

"Great. Her camp will be happy to hear that. I'll keep you up to date."

"All right, anything else? No? Okay, adjourned! Come on in, girls. I think we need some introductions, but first . . . ." d.dee took off her glasses, pulled Sarah down beside her and gave her a big kiss. d.dee felt it necessary to alter her appearance when she engaged in "intellectual pursuit," and conversely felt it as urgently necessary to remove the very same props when switching gears to romantic. When she studied, attended meetings, or offered workshops, she usually wore her small, oval wire glasses and braided her cinnamon hair into two inadequate, awkward braids. She didn't need glasses (except for the microscopic print in the two-volume OED that she had been given for Christmas); she just thought that they looked right. They looked intellectual.

If they hadn't had "posed" written all over them, Julie had often thought that those glasses had a chance of looking slightly sexy on d.dee. d.dee of all people! But d.dee ruined that chance because her artificial nonchalance was as inconspicuous as a neon-green shirt. There was no need to wear glasses. If you were smart, people knew it. If you were rich, people knew it. If you were drop-dead sexy, then absolutely everyone knew it and you were tired of talking about it. People were very well aware of what they thought you had over them.

"Okay, everybody, this is of course my on-again-off-again girlfriend, Sarah. Isn't she cute? And this is her best friend, Julie. This is Casey, eleven, (eleven's going to Berkley in the fall), and Sylvie. Jane and Dory had issues with the time, so either they'll come later or meet us at the bar."

"Hi," said Sarah as she began playfully swinging d.dee's arm back and forth.

"Hi, guys," said Julie.

d.dee shot a quick, apologetic glance at her friends. "Ummmm, Julie, not to be picky or anything and I've mentioned this before, but we don't like to be called guys, okay? Because we're not guys, we're girls, women actually. Could you respect that, please?"

"Oh, I'm sorry, it's a habit, d.dee. No disrespect intended."

"That's the problem, Julie," said d.dee. "Just a habit. If we can't even educate within our own ranks, then how can we expect to educate the rest of the world?"

"I don't know how," Julie said audibly and "Leave the rest of the world alone," she said inaudibly.

d.dee wrapped herself around Sarah. "I'm glad my girl is right here. All right, I'm starving, and I'm sure that everyone else is, too, so let's eat," commanded the boa constrictor.

The women politely filled their mismatched dishes and searched for adequate utensils. I think this is a grapefruit spoon, thought Julie. They took their food into the living room and sat enraptured around the tiny color television set.

"Oh my god, she's hot," said Casey.

"Oh god, I know," agreed d.dee. "I was always lousy at volleyball. You should have seen me trying to bump."

"God, I need a good, vigorous boink," said Sylvie.

"They're all on steroids," said Julie.

"I like the Chinese national anthem," said eleven. "It's one of the more melodic ones, though I do think that all national anthems should be abolished. By the way, d.dee, this chili is divine."

"Oh, do you really think so?" replied d.dee demurely. "I call it d.dee's Bowl of Compassion Vegetarian Chili. I got it off the Berkley web site, though I made a few modifications."

"Exquisite," said Sylvie. "Heavenly."

I could cut my tongue on this spoon, thought Julie.

Sylvie made a little moan. It was one of those little moans designed to make someone ask her what was wrong.

"What's wrong?" asked d.dee.

"Oh, sorry while we're eating and everything, it's just this damn yeast infection. It's flared up again."

"What are you doing for it?" asked d.dee.

"Well, I got medication from the pharmacist."

"Oh, most of those pharmacists have been brainwashed," said eleven. "Have you been drinking lots of water and cranberry juice?"

"Yes, but the juice is so expensive."

"True. Now here's one that perhaps you haven't heard of, but it's effective. It's a little more economical, and I vouch for it one hundred percent. Have you tried inserting yogurt into the vagina?"

"Yuck!" said Sarah and Sylvie simultaneously. Julie kept her head down.

"I know it sounds weird," eleven continued, "but trust me, it works."

"Isn't it rather messy?" asked Sylvie.

"It doesn't have to be. Use a recycled plastic tampon applicator or one you'd find in contraceptive foam. There's another way, too, which is kind of fun. You can make little Popsicles. You know those plastic molds your mom used when you were a kid? Well, you just put yogurt in those and freeze them and voila! Insert as needed. It's a little bit of a jolt at first of course, but nothing more so than jumping into a cold sauna after a hot one."

Nobody said much.

"Quite off the topic," continued eleven, "is anybody going to the Pugnit Rats next month?"

"The what? The who?" asked Julie now that she considered it safe to rejoin the conversation.

"The Pugnit Rats, the band?" said eleven looking at Julie like she couldn't believe that she had asked those questions.

"Sorry, I've never heard of them."

"Ohmigod, Julie," d.dee interjected. "They're my absolute favorite! They're only the hottest, multi-talented all-girl band *ever!* The members are from Portland and Seattle, Bill Gates country. That's where the name comes from. Pugnit Rats is 'Starting Up' backwards. Isn't that brilliant? And they're all gorgeous."

"Well, that's the thing, d.dee," said eleven. "Not too many people know about them. They put on one of the best live shows that I have ever seen, and I've seen them about five times. I've been a fan for years, before anyone ever heard of them."

* * * *

After the clean up, the girls began their pre-club preening. "That shirt looks great on you, Sarah," said Casey.

"Thanks."

"Oh no, even before we're out the door, she's getting compliments, never mind the fact that it's *my* shirt," said d.dee. She turned to Sarah and said, "Don't let it go to your head, dear."

"What, I can't even accept a compliment?"

"You don't accept compliments; you swallow them and become more of an insufferable flirt than you already are."

"What? I'm not a flirt!" replied Sarah with genuine indignation.

"Oh, you are so a terrible flirt. You're not even aware half the time that you're doing it."

"What? Julie, I'm a flirt?"

"I am not getting involved in this," Julie said and walked back into the bathroom to check her hair. It looked good tonight. It was the length Adrienne liked best, halfway between haircuts. Would she be there tonight?

"Thanks for the help," Sarah called after her.

"I'd say you were a flirt," piped up Sylvie. "You were flirting with me the first time we met."

"What? What's wrong with you people? Are you insane? I was just being nice, Sylvie. Have you both gone insane? I don't even think that way. That's your perception and it's off, totally off. You truly don't know what you're talking about. I was just chatting and being friendly and interested. I never look at a girl and think 'Oh, look at her over there, think I'll go over and flirt.' You have to meet people. I'm interacting socially. It's required, you know."

"It's *flirting*," said d.dee.

"Julie, come out here!" Sarah demanded.

Julie came out of the bathroom smoothing down her hair. "Well, I wouldn't say that it was one of your distinguishing characteristics myself, but I don't want to get in the middle of all this, so let's just go."

"Jane and Dory never called," said d.dee. "I guess they're just going to meet us there. Okay, I second the motion. Let's go."

* * * *

Casey parked the station wagon in the parking lot and the girls laughed their way across the alley into Rumors. It was a safe alley, not decrepit or dangerous, just south of the main downtown shopping area. It was women-only now, but it used to be a mixed club in the carefree pre-Aids days, and everybody still called it The Rear Entrance. On the street side was another bar for another kind of social misfit--a country and western nightclub. The shared walls provoked amusement and contempt from both sides.

The girls entered the bar into the ten o'clock atmosphere of optimistic expectation. Julie immediately began to scan the room for Adrienne and Meagan. Sarah pulled her along to a table against the wall, which was still open, and they commandeered it as a home base. Julie immediately went to the bar for a drink and stood in line. From there she could watch the door and the entire bar. She looked at every head, every bob and curl, every movement, but there was nothing familiar. Julie turned reluctantly and looked at the two bartenders. Even when it wasn't busy they moved with a controlled frantic motion. A girl with close-cropped, peroxide-blond hair came up to the bar, leaned over it and kissed one of them, Amy, possessively on the lips. At least early on in the evening, the way to make a bar full of dykes docile was to put them in a line waiting to be served by a beautiful bartender.

"Double vodka and Coke, a Bud Light, and two tequila shooters," said Julie with a big smile when it was her turn, nothing from Amy. If she hadn't turned and began precisely and efficiently pulling bottles from the mirrored shelves, Julie would have thought that she hadn't understood.

"Keep the change," said Julie. The bartender gave her a big smile.

"What'd you get me this for?" said Sarah as Julie put the shooter down in front of her.

"It's a present."

"You know what happens when I drink your presents."

"That's the point. Good, I haven't seen Heather. You don't see her anywhere, do you?"

"No, but I hardly remember what she looks like. I only saw her from behind at the party when she was with you. Oh, Julie, look at that girl in the white shirt on the dance floor," said Sarah.

"Yeah, she's cute."

They both turned and watched the girl dance. She occasionally leaned into her partner and whispered, then pulled back smiling. Her partner had long, black hair that she swished in a laborious, circular motion like a Kabuki actor in the 'Dance of the Shi-Shis.' Julie wondered if it was her girlfriend. They didn't touch like it. She remembered again that simple movement from shoulder to elbow. Julie closed her eyes and saw the movement of a hand down the length of Adrienne's arm.

The music stopped and brought Julie out of her reverie. The two girls also stopped dancing and waited to see what tune would come next. During that pause, the one in the white shirt scanned the crowd around the dance floor. Julie caught her eye for less than a second. The girl turned quickly away. Julie's heart went down. She needed another drink. Where was Sian? Julie flagged her over. Four tattoos, five piercings not counting ears, hair shaved to less than a millimeter, heavy black-booted, sweet Sian.

"Hi, hon. Long time no see! Nice to see you. What can I get for you?"

There was a long list.

"You know what the most important thing to do in a bar is, Sarah?" asked Julie as she sorted out the drinks.

"I know, Julie. You've told me a million times. Befriend the staff, especially the waiters or waitresses."

"Good, I am glad to see that you have been paying attention those million times. At least somebody listens to me. And what's the most important thing to tell the waitress?"

"Whatever she does, to please, please, please don't forget to tell you when it's last call."

"Excellent, Grasshopper."

"Hey, Jules. There she is again. Go on." Sarah clinked her glass against Julie's. "Ask her to dance. Nothing to lose."

"Everything to lose."

"Nothing to lose! Stop thinking about the phone call! Give yourself a break, and have a good time. Ask her to dance."

"No," Julie shook her head gravely. "There's a lot to lose. Nothing to lose is how we, the desperate and pathetic, convince ourselves to do something that we know is futile. We want to be pushed into it."

"Okay, I'm pushing you. Just go on."

"Okay. You think I should? Okay."

Holding her precious drink above her head, Julie squeezed and 'excused me'd' herself circuitously counter-clockwise through the packed bar and came up to the girl from her left. She mustered a big smile and said, "Hello."

"Hello," returned the girl.

"Would you like to dance?"

"Oh, not right now," said White Shirt and looked at her friend. "I just came off the dance floor. I need a bit of a breather, but thanks anyway. Maybe later."

"Okay," said Julie. To White Shirt's Shi-Shi dancing friend she knew better than to say, "Well, then, how about you, then?" Whose idea had it been to come to this stupid place, anyway? Humiliated, Julie inched her way back over to the bar and stood in line. She ordered two double vodka and Cokes and a round of B-52 shooters and took them back to the table.

"I'm sorry," said Sarah when she got back.

"Just forget it. You have to go to the bathroom again?"

"No."

Julie walked to the ladies' room and joined the line. There were five girls in front of her and three stalls, actually two stalls because the middle one was out of order. Only once in all the years that Julie had been coming to Rumors was it not out of order. What the fuck was taking them so long in there? Finally the stall at the far end opened and two girls spilled out sniffing, laughing, and wiping their noses. They washed their hands and checked themselves alertly in the mirror. They turned to leave when one of them saw her and said, "Julie!"

"Hey, Shelley. Now, what took you so long in there?"

"Wouldn't you like to find out? Hey, where are you sitting?"

"Over there with Sarah and company. Come over after."

"Yeah, I've got something to tell you."

"Okay. I'll be waiting."

"There anything on my face, Jules?"

"No, you're okay."

＊ ＊ ＊ ＊

Julie returned to the table just as a sweaty, breathless d.dee was returning to the table to retrieve her Evian. "Who were you dancing with, honey?" asked Sarah.

"Oh, that was Kylie Terrell. She is the new national president of the Scully Fan Club. They're trying to get Gillian Anderson here for a dinner next year."

"Wow!" gushed Sarah. "Has she met her?"

"Yup, twice. Shook her hand even."

"No way! Wow! I'll go. I'll go!"

Julie joined the conversation. "It's a new generation, that's for sure," she said flatly. "Raised on *X-Files*. Scully is to this generation what Lindsay Wagner was to my generation. *The Bionic Woman*, Jaime Sommers. Remember, you guys?"

"Of course," said d.dee.

"She was beautiful, but young women these days don't know who you're talking about. And someday, though it's hard to believe right now, even Scully will be replaced."

"Scully will never be replaced!" cried d.dee.

"That's right," agreed Sarah, "never."

"Don't count on it, girls. I don't see what's so great about Gillian Anderson anyway. Wasn't she a POR-NO actress before?"

"Not so great? How can you say that! She's gorgeous!" defended Sarah. "Oh, her nose, her lips, her eyes. How can you say that?"

"She is beautiful, Julie," agreed d.dee. "She wasn't a porno actress either, that's a myth catalyzed by envy. Her erotic work was just paying her dues, getting famous. Who hasn't done that?"

"You mean erotic work paying her dues like Pam Anderson? Watch Pam suck Tommy Lee's massive cock? You despise Pam, then why not Scully? What if Pam was the star of *X-Files* and Gillian the star of *Baywatch*?"

"Look, Julie, shut up, will you? And for your information, Pam and Tommy's video was *after* she was famous. I don't care if you like Scully or not. I think she's a babe. That's all. Anyway, with you out of the way there is less competition for me."

"What if she's not vegetarian?"

"She probably is."

"How would you know? I bet she's not. Then what would you do?"

"Well, regrettably, I couldn't date her then. I absolutely cannot be with someone who does not share my value system. Period."

"Oh right. I'm sure that if Gillian Anderson walked through that door right now and got down on her knees in front of you and begged, begged,

begged you to go out with her that you would refuse her on those grounds."

"I'd change her then."

"d.dee," said Sarah, "I really don't appreciate it you sitting here talking about other women that you'd like to fuck in front of me."

"I'm sorry, honey." d.dee put both hands on Sarah's face and pulled her close. "After you of course, honey, after you. Scully's my second choice. You're always the first. You know that. Anyway, you just said yourself how gorgeous she is."

"Well, I just said 'gorgeous.' I didn't say anything about 'less competition' or changing her now, did I? There's a big difference in saying that you find someone attractive and in saying that you're after them right in front of your girlfriend."

"Honey, I would only fuck Scully *after* we were for sure broken up. You can trust me on that."

Sarah pulled away and crossed her arms in front of her chest and said nothing.

d.dee put her arm around Sarah's shoulders and squeezed. "I love only you, baby, only you. And you know, after watching you two, I feel like a shooter myself. Julie, you're good at it. See if you can get Sian's attention." To Julie's disgust, d.dee pronounced it "shone."

"It's not 'shone' as in 'I shone my flashlight,' d.dee. It's pronounced 'Sian' as in 'see-on.'"

"That's not the way I've heard it."

Julie rested her elbow on the table and leaned into d.dee. "Well, you've heard it wrong then, and trust me it's not the first time in your repertoire. Ask her yourself. I should know. I'm one of her best customers."

"No, I'm not asking her. She's too gorgeous."

"I bet she likes old-fashioned fairy tales. I'm gonna ask her when she comes over."

"Go to hell, Julie. Who's the mirror in Snow White? Who's deciding? And Disney *destroyed* that story by giving the dwarves names and personalities. There are better ways to entertain, Julie, better messages to send, better stories to tell. We've also been working on our own collection of fairy tales. Of course you've neglected to inquire about that."

"You're writing fairy tales?"

"Yes. We are currently working on a volume of modern, inoffensive gender-equitable fairy tales. And you know even still calling them 'fairy tales' is discriminatory. However, we haven't been able to agree on an alternative term yet. We'll have it soon, though."

"Oh, god, d.dee, you make me so thirsty." It was time for Julie to escape the table for another tray of shooters. She made her way through the crowd of women to the bar. Once there, she decided to nix the tray of shooters and order a vodka straight. When the bartender brought it, she ordered another, and without returning to the table, she downed both of them. She looked across the bar at White Shirt and her new ponytailed pal. Her earlier humiliation began to transform into a dark determination. So if Adrienne didn't want her, didn't love her, at least she could get this girl tonight. If Adrienne wasn't going to show up and do her part, Julie was still easily attractive enough to get a substitute for the evening. She again pushed her way over to the two women.

"Hi, it's later," said Julie as she approached White Shirt. "I didn't introduce myself last time, my name's Julie." She held out her hand. The girl gave Julie's fingers a brief, limp shake with an unenthusiastic, damp hand.

"Hi, I'm Holly."

Julie clasped Holly's hand and held it tightly. "Well, how about that dance, Holly?" she asked perkily.

"Oh, I'm really not in the mood. I have to be in the mood to dance."

"Oh, come on, just one li'l dance won't kill ya."

Holly exchanged smug looks with the girl beside her. The girl, with whom she had been dancing and then necking with merely minutes ago, had a tight, not-very-long, blond ponytail sticking crookedly up from the top of her head. She danced with a rigid stutter making her look as if she were receiving minor doses of electrocution.

"Well, actually, I am kind of in the middle of a conversation right now," said Holly and gently tried to pull her hand away. Julie didn't let go.

"Yeah, we're kind of in the middle of something," piped up Ponytail primly.

"Nonsense," said Julie. "Now what you two need ta do is loosen up a li'l, ladies. Whydda have ta drink? My treat!"

Holly finally freed her hand. "We're fine, but thanks anyway." She turned to Ponytail with her back to Julie.

"Okay, I'll get 'em, just hold on," said Julie. There is a state of alcohol saturation that renders even the most blatant social snub completely impotent. Julie flagged down Sian. "What're those two lovely ladies behind me drinkin', sweetheart?" She reached out and rubbed Sian's head.

"One's gin and tonic and the other's a virgin Caesar."

"Uh huh, that figures. That would be Ponytail. 'Nuther round please for them and mine's a double vodka Coke. Just bring them to Shelley's table."

After she had paid Sian and stroked her head once again, Julie picked up the gin and tonic and Caesar and walked up behind the two women.

"Here you are, ladies."

They turned and looked at her expressionlessly as she held out the glasses to them. "Well, come on, take 'em. They're paid for."

They hesitated and then awkwardly took the drinks and set them on the shelf beside them.

"Now hold on, I gotta get mine. Couldn't carry it -- not a waitress! Hold on, don't go anywhere." Julie scurried back to Shelley's table and grabbed her full-to-the-rim, cold vodka and Coke and stumbled back to the women. "A toast. Cheers, Shriner. Anybody's dad drive a little car?" She took a drink and slopped a little down the front of her shirt. The duo took reluctant sips and said nothing.

"Look," said Ponytail. "I'm not trying to be rude here . . . I'm sorry I forgot, what was your name again?"

"I don't believe that we were ever formally introduced. Julie is my name." God, did Julie want to belt her.

"Okay, Julie, we really are trying to have a conversation, a *private* conversation."

Julie hadn't liked the look of her from the beginning. This tight, erect Ponytail in a tee shirt and low-slung jeans held up with a thick, black belt had irritated her from the second she had laid eyes on her. "In a bar?" Julie asked. "There are better places to have private conversations, but speakin' of private conversations, I'd like to have one myself. If you'll excuse us," she said and pulled Holly off to the side. She whispered half in Holly's ear and half in her hair, "So, ya want me to get rid of her and you can't say it? Jus gimme some secret sign, wink or something."

"No," said Holly. "That's fine."

"Okay then . . . ." Julie paused and concentrated very hard for a few seconds. "So, she's your cousin?"

"No, she's not my cousin."

"Kissing cousins." Julie again paused looking like someone determined to mine the answer to a tricky riddle. "So ya just don't wanna dance with me, iz that right? That's the bottom line? Just tell me and I'll go away, bottom line. Not a stalker, you know. Mmmm not trying to pick you up or sommen, jus wanted n' innocent dance, not trying to marry you or sommen. It's your prerogative and Julie Bell knows where and when she's not wanted, you only hafta tell Julie Bell once. Bottom line, that's it."

"That's right, bottom line, no dancing, I'm sorry, Julie." Julie didn't move.

"Meaning . . . meaning . . . ." and she flicked her wrist to gesture in the direction of Ponytail and spilled more of her drink over her hand, jeans, and shoes, "that you'd rather dance with her? So yer choosin her," and this time she pointed dramatically at Ponytail. "Well, iz there sommen wrong with me or sommen? Adrienne sure thinks so; you're not the only one who thinks so, ask Adrienne. You don't like me or sommen, izzazt right? I don't know why yoooooooooou don't like me. I like yoooooou."

"I like you, Julie. I just don't know you. I was talking to her first."

"To her? No, no you werren, yer, yer with yer other shi-shi friend before. I saw ya before Ponytail showed up, looooong before Ponytail showed up on the scene. I saw ya first, first dibs. Whatiz wrong with me?

Why don't you love me? I love yoooou." Julie lifted her glass to her lips, but it slipped in her grip and watery Coke and vodka sprinkled on her and Holly.

"God," said Holly angrily. "Goodbye!" She turned back to The Erection.

"Fine then, jus fine for you, Fat Cats," Julie said to Holly's back and sloshed away. "Faaat Cats, they'll be sorry."

Ponytail glared after her with the kind of look that she gave when she tried to park her racing-green sport utility in front of the health food store and someone's car was hogging too much space. "Disgusting," she said.

* * * *

"Disgusting, disgusting." Julie repeated Ponytail's words to herself as she surveyed the stain on her shirt. Yes, she was. Drunk, humiliated, stained inside and out. She never should have come here. She started to stumble toward the entrance when someone grabbed her arm. It was Shelley.

"So, listen," began Shelley. "How you been doing lately? Still pretty raw?"

"Yup, pretty raw, Shel. Whaz up?"

"I wanted to ask you if anything was going on?"

"Going on?"

"With Adrienne."

"Adrienne? Whaddya mean?"

"Well, they were here earlier."

"Adrienne and Meagan?"

"Yeah, and it was pretty dead early so you could see everything going on."

Everything going on, Shelley went on to relate that Meagan and Adrienne had come in looking like they had intended to stay out all night. However, at one point, Meagan had pulled a girl from Shelley's table up to dance while Adrienne was at the bar. When Adrienne returned, she saw Meagan and the girl on the dance floor kissing. Understandably, she stomped off. Meagan came flying after her apologizing, telling her that she was just doing it to make her jealous, and that it had worked too well. Meagan had said that is was obviously staged because she hadn't had nearly enough to drink to make it real and that she just liked to make her partners' jealousy flare occasionally.

"It was quite a spectacle, Jules. Anyway, they ended up leaving right after that. Let me tell you, Meagan's in the doghouse. Are they having problems?"

Julie's turbulent mind was having problems. She couldn't process the new information and categorize it neatly. Her mind began to whirl faster. Her stomach began to inch up to meet it. She felt cold. "Thanks. Thanks, Shelley. I gotta go." Julie made her way desperately through the faces and bodies that blocked her progress. A few saw and instinctively opened a path. Julie hit the bathroom, but the vomit began to come up and spill all over the floor before she reached the porcelain sink.

Chapter 11 - An Unfortunate Wedding

The pip of the ace of spades is a shadow that gets bigger and smaller, like its height is being adjusted on a radio frequency. Meagan is twisting the knob furiously as she tries to find the station. The static drills into my head. I have to wake up. I can't wake up. I have to wake up! The pressure is crushing my head!

Sarah peeked into the bedroom. "Bad dream?"

"Yes."

Julie lay still. Even without a massive hangover, waking up was invariably excruciating. It was something that she'd never gotten the hang of. She wondered how long it would take until she woke up and automatically thought of something besides Adrienne dumping her. Please, she thought, just let my mind clasp onto something else within the first seconds of consciousness. Please rush the inevitable healing when that memory would be replaced with something innocuous: a trip, a dog, anything else. No more knots.

How different would her life have been if she had gotten up early like a cow milker? If she had trained herself to be productive in the peaceful early hours before too many people woke up and confused things. If she had forced herself to smile no matter how she was feeling and jumped out of bed at 4 a.m. like the news anchors?

"I let myself in to do some laundry," said Sarah. "You didn't answer the phone, so I just came over."

"Are you doing d.dee's laundry in this house, too?"

"No."

"Let me see your laundry."

"It's already in the washer."

"I'm gonna check it when it comes out."

"Just some panties and a couple pairs of jeans. Well, didn't someone wake up on the wrong side of the bed this morning? At least you made it to your bed. What time did you get home anyway?"

"Just some panties. What are you, twelve? What are you doing tonight, little girl? I'm having a sleepover with my girlfriends in our panties. Don't know, ended up going to a party with Shelley and some of her friends. Sarah, something big is happening! Maybe."

"What?"

"There's big trouble between Adrienne and you-know-who."

"No, really?"

"Yup! Meagan's in the dog house for kissing some girl in front of her, trying to make her jealous. How mature. That bitch."

"No way!"

"Way! I can't remember everything Shel said right now. I have to process some more. What about you? You have a good time?"

"As a matter of fact, I did. You disappeared and d.dee left early-- we're off again--and then I met a really nice girl. We ended up going to Denny's for coffee."

"Off again? You were so lovey-dovey at dinner, what happened?"

"I think it started with the Scully thing. Never mind, I don't want to go into it."

"All right, I don't really want to hear about it anyway. You ended up going out with someone for coffee?"

"Yup."

"That's great! What's her name?"

"Erica."

"She cute?"

"Very. She's a fine arts student and she works part-time at the university library."

"Are you going to see her again?"

"Well, we weren't actually 'seeing' each other. We just ended up there because her friend is a waitress there and she can get a discount."

"She needs a discount on coffee?"

"She's a student. It was just conversation."

"Well, are you not going to have a date and flirt with her again?"

"I admit it. I hope I see her. She's really cute. Hold on, I gotta put the clothes in the dryer. You have anything that you want me to wash?"

"No, that's okay, thanks . . . no, wait." Julie reached under the covers. "Do my panties, will you?"

The delicious complicity connected to the possible betrayal of d.dee proved a remarkable hangover cure. Julie felt instantly better. She heard the steady, low rumble of the dryer. She listened to the washing machine filling with water that muffled instantaneously when the lid was closed. Sarah came back into her room and sprawled at the end of her bed.

"She actually did invite me to go to an exhibition with her."

"An exhibition?"

"Yeah. There's a Max Ernst exhibition at Gallery Ueda that we both want to see."

"Max Ernst? Who's that? Sounds familiar but . . . ."

"He was one of the Surrealist painters, came to America to escape from the Nazis. He was married to Peggy Guggenheim for a while."

"Okay, but I still really don't know."

"Oh, he was incredible. I'm reading a biography of Peggy Guggenheim right now. Interesting family, the Guggenheims."

"Rich."

"Peggy's father went down on the *Titanic,* and the biographer says that her mother used to repeat things three times, like 'you should wear this dress, this dress, this dress.'"

"Well," said Julie. "I don't know much about art, but it sounds interesting."

"You know, d.dee would never go to this exhibition. First, because he's a man, and second because she thinks he was lousy to women. That's only one side of the story. Who knows? If I were a famous painter, I'd try to get as many beautiful women as I could, too. What's wrong with that?"

"Oh, how does she know anything? Like she knows anything that went on. That's what I've been saying all this time, Sarah. I'm sorry, but don't you get tired of it? You must be tired of all the exclusions, the exclusions, the exclusions."

Since Adrienne left, Julie had been thinking a lot about exclusions, the exclusions or the atomization of modern ways, but it really didn't matter much anyway what she kept in or tried to keep out; she always ended up getting blindsided by something unexpected.

"She's a good person."

"I'm not saying that she isn't, Sarah. I'm talking about the exclusions. Since Adrienne dumped me, every judgment seems more futile than ever. You know that it's not just d.dee, but everyone. It's me, too. We say that we could never date someone who ate meat or someone who smoked, or we couldn't possibly live with someone who hated *The Simpsons*. Are they really values? What does it say about us that we don't instead say that we couldn't possibly date someone who was emotionally destructive or apathetic or paralyzed? We don't tolerate cruelty to animals, but we sure as hell tolerate it toward humans."

"Good points, Julie. Let me think about it. I can't answer right now. So, do you think it would be cheating if I went with Erica?"

"Absolutely not! Last night you were technically separated again, so guilt erased, please."

"Why do I feel like I'm doing something wrong, then?"

"Because you're a sweet and loyal girlfriend, that's why. You have done absolutely nothing wrong. Go out and enjoy yourself. This whole separation thing was entirely d.dee's idea, remember."

"You're right," Sarah said, sounding not convinced. She pulled the end of the bedspread up and wrapped herself in it. "She is soooo cute. I can just imagine her putting the books on the shelves, pushing the little cart. She was in my dream last night already. Oh, good! That reminds me. I have been meaning to tell you. I had a dream last week, and I know it's just a dream, but I have to warn you about it anyway."

"What?"

"Okay, I dreamt that you were taking care of Persephone for me while I was on vacation."

"Where did you go?"

"Shut up . . . can't remember, maybe Greece."

"Oh, I want to go to Greece."

"Anyway, I called you to check on her and you said that she had seemed a little sluggish, but not to worry because you had ground up a Tylenol and put it in her food and she seemed much better. I know it's just a dream, but you know not to give Tylenol to cats, right? Or any animal, right?"

"Of course I know that . . . I give 'em aspirin."

"That's not funny."

"I know!"

"Okay, I'm just checking, sorry. Had to be sure."

The phone rang and Julie stretched to the side of the bed, reached down and took the pillow off the extension on the floor and answered.

"Hi."

"Hi, Sarah over there?"

"Who's calling, please?"

"Let me speak to her, please?"

"I'm sorry, it's whoooo?"

"Julie!"

"It's Julie calling?"

"Julie, come off it."

"I apologize Miss, but to transfer your call would be to violate the terms of an agreed upon trial separation, and I for one will not be a party to . . . ."

"Julie, put her on the phone!"

"One moment please, Miss."

"Ms. Brooks, from what I can discern, you're wanted on the telephone by a rather hostile Miss Julie or someone who refuses to give her name. I tried my best to dissuade her, but she's a feisty one."

"Hi, hon, how are you?" said Sarah into the phone as she grinned at Julie.

"Oh really? I've never heard anything about that, no way . . . really? Oh, I'm so sorry, hon. Oh, baby . . . . Well, I am doing laundry right now. Hold on a sec." Sarah covered the mouthpiece with her hand and turned to Julie. "Is it okay if d.dee comes over? She really needs some company right now."

"Sure," said Julie irritably. Her hangover suddenly returned full force.

"Thanks. Hon, why don't you come on over to Julie's and hang out with us 'til I finish the laundry? Then we can do something fun. It's okay, baby. It'll be all right. Come on, see you soon." She hung up the phone scowling.

Sarah so rarely scowled that, when she did, it was much more potently expressive than on most people. Julie thought that she hadn't seen that genre of scowl on Sarah before, ever. The displeasure on her face now seemed calibrated much higher than the regular d.dee-induced frowns. Her forehead wrinkled in the middle in a way that Julie had not seen during the routine disagreements that punctuated her and d.dee's relationship.

"What's wrong now?" asked Julie. "Her Spotlight on Prozac support group disband? I can't believe that she'd still want to come over here, especially after last night. I really laid into her, didn't I?"

"d.dee's a forgiving person," said Sarah who, with a slight smile replacing the scowl, was back to looking like herself. Still, it was a tentative smile. "You never give her credit for that."

"Whatever. I'm going to ask you again, and one of these times I am going to get a definitive answer. What's the point of a trial separation if you aren't going to abide by the restrictions?"

"This is important. It's an exception. What do you have to drink? I'm thirsty."

"Go look. I don't think there's much, but I could use something myself."

As Sarah went into the kitchen, Julie lifted herself slowly off the bed. She opened her sock drawer and stared zombie-like into the jumble of pudgy sock balls and cotton underwear, but couldn't fathom why she had opened it, so she closed it without taking anything out. She remained standing in front of the dresser staring at nothing. A couple of minutes later she opened the drawer beneath the sock drawer and pulled out a wrinkled white tee shirt. Next, she took a pair of folded jeans from the middle drawer and threw them on the bed. Then, she went back to the sock drawer. This time she pulled out a pair of short, white socks, and a pair of navy men's boxer shorts. She sat back down on the bed because she felt dizzy and nauseous. Maybe she wasn't ready to venture out just yet. She lay back down clutching her change of clothes on her chest. She needed some hangover food. "I need a McChicken or a Quarter Pounder, fries and a Coke," she mumbled. "I gotta get my hands on that."

Sarah brought her in a glass of grape juice and then left her alone. Julie lay still another twenty minutes.

Again she attempted to get up and get dressed. If it were possible, she moved even slower this time. Avoid jerky movements, she thought. She closed her eyes as she pulled on her clothes because she would rather not have a look at her body today. Cautiously, like a frail grandmother, she padded into the bathroom, picked up her fluorescent purple toothbrush, squeezed a liberal amount of toothpaste onto it, dipped it under the tap and started brushing. Even though she knew that she was supposed to turn off the water while she brushed, she didn't. Wasting enough water that would supply an entire African village could not deter her because she was just so lazy today. Besides that, she could barely move her wrist. Every drop down the drain was one less drop for . . . Sarah's distorted, muffled voice interrupted her self-chastising thoughts.

"Jeezus Christ." She turned off the water and waited. Silence. She waited some more, then turned the water back on and resumed brushing. Again came Sarah's voice. "Jeezus!" She angrily twisted the faucet off, spit, grabbed a towel to wipe her mouth and then flung the door open.

"*What* did you say?"

"I said, 'I'm using your iiiiron.'"

"You just have to wait 'til I go to the bathroom, close the door and start running the water and brushing my teeth to tell me that, don't you? The moment I have impaired my hearing to the maximum is what you're waiting for, isn't it? Couldn't you just tell me that while I was lying down?"

"Sorry. I just started now."

"Couldn't you have waited until I was finished, or was it that important? I can't hear you in here!"

"I'm sorry. I just don't like using things without asking, even here. I'm sorry."

"Just please try to pay more attention on mornings like these, okay?"

"Okay."

"I'm going to McDonalds. You want something?"

"Is breakfast still on?"

"I don't think so."

"Well, nothing then, but if it is, bring me some hash browns."

"Okay, sorry for being a bitch."

"It's okay. Sorry for annoying you."

"That's okay. There's a possibility that I annoy you at times, too."

* * * *

Julie carried the cardboard tray protectively to the entrance, pushed open the door, and walked back into the sunshine. It was hard to concentrate on formulating social policy like a McDonalds draft to improve the character of young people when all you wanted to do was rip open a paper bag and stuff a hamburger into your mouth. She unrolled the bag and daintily took out a long, warm, golden fry, popped it into her mouth, and then rolled the bag back up. "Yum." She unrolled the bag again and took out two more. That was it until she got home. Okay, just one more. Recently Julie preferred to eat her orders in the car or at home. Since the children's play area was usually packed, and since Julie was usually nursing one, it was the best decision for everyone involved. It wasn't only that the rambunctious children could set her off, it was that she was likely to become irritable and uncomfortable with the vultures hanging around with their trays just waiting to pounce on her seat milliseconds after she vacated it. It really wasn't the restaurant for an alcoholic lingerer.

Julie pawed her pockets for her keys at the front door of her apartment building. Jeezus why did they always end up in her left pocket? Then, she either had to take them out with her weak hand and transfer them, or reach across Twister-style with her right hand to her left pocket. She supposed that she should train herself to open the door with her left hand; it would only be an asset. From now on she was going to make a concentrated effort to put her keys only in her right-hand pocket. The left pocket would be boycotted. Instead of waiting for the elevator, Julie sprinted up the stairs to her apartment. She had intended to take her treasure to her room and eat and read on the bed, but was severely annoyed to find that her bedroom door was closed.

"What the hell?"

Sarah came out with a serious look on her face.

"Hi, Julie," she said in a low tone. "I'm sorry. Don't get angry, okay? d.dee's in there, and she's very upset. I thought it best to put her in there so she'd be out of your hair. Don't worry. I tidied up all your stuff first. You can watch TV and move around out here. Is it okay?"

"I guess so. Like I have a choice." She shook her head and slapped the bag down on the table. "What's going on now?"

"It's kind of a crisis."

"It's *always* a crisis with her. What's wrong this time?"

"Didn't you hear yet?"

"Hear what?"

"Ani DiFranco got married."

Julie laughed. "So?"

"To a man."

"So?"

"So, you know d.dee's a huge fan. She has the web site. She put a lot of work into it."

"Well, can't she be a huge fan if Ani's married?"

"Of course she can, but she just feels betrayed. Ani let down the women's community that has supported her all these years."

"She didn't betray anyone. It's not her fault that the lesbian community put the vise grip on her. Leave the woman alone for god's sake. She's done more than her share."

"Well, that's not the main reason anyway. The main reason is that the music's changed so much from the early days that d.dee's decided to shut down the site. It was a major decision for her. It's like the loss of a loved one."

"I don't have time for this bullshit. All right, whatever you say. Look, I just want to eat in peace. Oh, by the way," she said as Sarah headed back into the bedroom, "for the prevention of future heartbreak, you'd better tell d.dee that Scully's married . . . to a man."

Julie arranged some pillows on the floor and reached for the remote control. Later, d.dee and Sarah emerged. A plaintive and meek d.dee said, "I really appreciate you letting me take over your space, Julie. I apologize for the inconvenience."

"That's okay." d.dee's eyes were bloodshot and there were dark crescents under them.

"Fry?" Julie asked d.dee as she dabbed one into the small mound of ketchup on the corner of the laid out wrapper. "Only a couple left."

"No, thanks."

"Sarah?"

"Don't mind if I do."

Julie thought of bringing up last night's exchange, but d.dee truly looked too weak to harass and Julie only took it up with people she believed could take it.

"We're gonna take off, Julie," said Sarah. "Thanks for everything."

"Sure."

"Yeah, thanks," said d.dee. "Oh, by the way. Is there something wrong between Adrienne and Meagan? I heard . . . ."

"Let's just say, d.dee, that the voodoo spell has finally been broken. Let's just say that Adrienne has finally come to her senses and realized what most people have known all along. You two take care."

"We will. Bye," said Sarah.

Julie finished her feast, pulled the pillows down from against the wall, grabbed the afghan, covered herself and went blissfully to sleep.

Chapter 12 - Red Herrings

"Listen to this." Sarah read, "'Under the guise of a medical examination, impoverished Turks are being lured to India where one of their kidneys is removed for black market organ sales.' Can you believe that?"

"You've got to be pret-ty stupid to fall for that."

"Or desperate. These things happen."

"I'd like to think very rarely. Just how do you swindle a kidney out of someone anyway, Sarah? It's hard to comprehend who the people are in the world that fall for these things. Would you fall for it, even if you were impoverished? I mean, there has to be a point when you realize that this isn't looking like manual labor and you get out of there, no? Like you know how you're not supposed to go to someone's uncle's house for coffee and a card game in Southeast Asia, or the swindled seniors on those lottery scams? I can't fathom it. At least I've scared my grandmother sufficiently so that she won't even buy a scratch ticket now. How much does a kidney go for these days anyway? How much do you think I could get for one of mine?"

"People are paying thousands of dollars. Of course, the Turks don't see that kind of money. They get only a fraction of that. It's not the same here, though. A friend of a friend of d.dee's flew to Scotland to give her cousin a kidney and you wouldn't believe what she had to go through. She had to have psychological tests done by three different doctors, and then the surgery was postponed twice. The whole thing was stalled by bureaucracy while they made sure that she wasn't doing it just for the money. Can you imagine her poor cousin? He was deteriorating the entire time, but that was secondary to them. So, you'd better think twice if you ever consider something like that. It's not an easy, foolproof, money-making scheme."

"I wasn't serious, Sarah. Organ sales, transplants, technology; what a time in history we live in, hey? Things are advancing so fast that there aren't even laws to cover all the new areas. I was reading about that in *The Washington Post* last week. Say, for example, frozen embryos . . . ."

"Frozen embryos."

"Smart ass. In the case of a divorce, who gets the embryos?"

"Yeah, I never would have thought of that. That's a tough one. Since d.dee started explaining some stuff to me though, I'm not comfortable with any of the advances in reproductive technology anymore. I used to support it, but it all kind of gives me the creeps now. As a matter of fact, d.dee is thinking of starting a group against cloning. It may be the first time in her life that she agrees with the Religious Right."

"Against cloning? Why?"

"It's just a strong personally-held belief of hers. She doesn't want the possibility of any of her friends or family, and obviously herself, ever being subjected to something like that. Our life here on earth is very precious and cannot be duplicated."

"I have just one question to ask you, Sarah."

"What's that?"

"Who would clone your girlfriend?"

Sarah nodded thoughtfully.

"Don't tell me that she really thinks that whoever's in charge of cloning out there, out of the billions of people to choose from on the earth, is going to have *her* at the top of their list? And besides, it's a totally irrational, bizarre fear. You don't just clone in the lab and then, wham, the whole army of clones takes over the world! Isn't there going to be at least one disgruntled clone to expose the entire operation? It's inane to be afraid of this."

"I'm not talking to you."

"Here, let me consult the Clone Master List. Ah, yes, bring on the former Karen Kaufman . . . ."

"Shut up."

"Okay, but what I was saying before about the embryos; someone's gotta figure all this stuff out. I should have been on the Supreme Court. Now that would be an interesting job. A significant job."

* * * *

"Hello, Meagan? It's Julie."

"What the hell do you want? You've got a lot of nerve."

"I just wanted to say that I am sorry for calling there drunk." Meagan was silent. She hadn't been expecting this crafty, straightforward-sincere-apology approach, so she needed time to turn it into something that she could attack.

"Well, you should be." Buying time.

"I swear, I don't remember, and I will never do that again."

"You'd better not."

"I won't. And I wasn't trying to be rude to Brenda at the party, either. I apologize if it came across that way."

"It sounded rude to me."

Contriteness has a limit. She had expected Meagan to accept the apology. "Well, I'm sorry if that's the way it came across." She spoke with her mouth drawn in tight as she tried to hold in the building impatience and anger. "It wasn't meant that way. I was just trying to help. I do know a little bit about publishing, by the way. My uncle's in publishing."

"You were showing disrespect to my cousin." Meagan was cruising now.

"Disrespect?" Julie's voice rose. "That doesn't even enter into it. I was only trying to dissuade her from writing an autobiography that, even if by some miracle she got published, no one would buy."

"There you go again, more insults."

"They're not insults! I am talking about true markets here, the survival of the fittest and all that. Who is going to buy the book, Meagan? Who? Who? Tell me. Tell me."

"Sure, I'll tell you something. Why don't you go fuck yourself? Which I'm sure you do a lot of these days."

"Use some more swear words while you're at it."

"The only words appropriate in this case, you bitch."

"They're red herrings, you know."

"What?"

"Red herrings. It's when you don't have the skill or intelligence to debate or argue legitimately, and all you can do is resort to flinging low-class vulgarities, which are off the topic completely. I make an intelligent comment regarding publishing, but you're unable to reply with anything equally intelligent, so your primitive, uneducated reply is something like 'Fuck you,' or 'So what, you're fat.' They're called red herrings. You should know what you're expert at. Why don't you let Brenda stand on her own two feet for once instead of using her all the time?"

"Fuck you. You don't know anything about being an artist."

"An artist. You think you're an artist? That's laughable. Under what genre would I find your so-called films in the video shop, Meagan? 'Contrived?'"

"I'm gonna fucking kill you. Adrienne is mine, and it was too easy to get her away from you, you loser, you worthless piece of . . . ."

"Tell Brenda that I'll be watching the New York Times Best Seller list closely," Julie said and slammed down the phone.

Julie stood mutely staring at the phone and wondered: How did *that* happen? She had phoned with the best intentions, with compassion and an apology on her mind, and how did that happen, that divergence from the path? Could it be reduced to that simple axiom that she had heard so often recently, "Don't have any expectations"? Don't have any expectations? That would be like asking her not to breathe.

* * * *

"I don't know how I let you talk me into these things, Sarah."

"Usually I'm the one saying that to you, Julie. I let you talk me into things all the time. Return the favor for once. If you're not having a good time, you can always cut it short after the movie. You're adults. You can figure that part out. Now don't go in there with a negative attitude because then for sure you won't have a good time. Try to think a little positively for once, okay? It will really do you some good. This is so great that you're finally doing it!"

"I must have been crazy to have been talked into this." Julie threw the comb into the bathroom sink and stormed back into her bedroom. "Now that it comes right down to it, this whole blind date scene really freaks me out."

Sarah picked the comb out of the sink and followed Julie back into her bedroom. "It's not a 'blind' date. You've seen her before."

"Okay, a near-sighted one, then. I saw her for about forty-five seconds when she came in and handed something to you and left."

"But you thought that each other were cute. That's the point. That's how things happen. It's the starting point, Julie. Turn around." Sarah began combing Julie's hair at the back.

"I think you're cute, too. Does that mean that we should date?"

"Sometimes these things work out really well, and you just might be thanking me big time someday."

Julie pulled away and lay down on her bed and put a pillow over her head. She couldn't get Adrienne out of her head. How could she possibly make a step towards anyone else?

Sarah sat on the edge. "Don't! You'll ruin your hair, my creation! Jules, the hard part's over. You've seen each other and approved, so all that anxiety disappears. Calls have been made; details have been worked out. Now you've both just got to show and be your single, available, charming selves."

"You mean 'the dating self,' preceding 'the real me.' And she's not single. She's still with Carmen."

"No, they are taking a break from each other right now. Debbie has even moved out, gotten her own place."

"I'd prefer someone with no one else in the picture, and you've mentioned that they've done this before, too. I don't like the sound of it now that I think about it some more."

"Why? She wouldn't be going out if they were firmly together."

"Because some women use it to make their girlfriends jealous – Hello, Meagan! -- or to provoke some other kind of reaction. It's not even a real date then; it's a scheme. I'm going on a scheme, Sarah. I just don't like the feel of it. Julie the willing pawn, Julie the desperate, willing pawn, and everybody knows it."

"What?"

"And let's not forget the fact that Carmen is a horrible-tempered power lifter, too. She could snap me in half. Snap me like a twig. Their relationship is just a string of episodes. Now we're having the 'Julie Episode.'"

"Get up. It's too late. She'll be on her way there. I will push you out the door if necessary. And don't forget to use her name often like I told you."

"What was that again?"

"Say her name a lot. It's one of Dale Carnegie's six steps--making your counterpart feel important."

"Really? That's one of them? That's so simple. I have always imagined them being more complex than that."

"No, that's the beauty of the course and why it has endured over the years. It's simplicity. Simple, universal truths to improve human communication."

"Jeez, you sound like a commercial for them or something."

"No, I just remember that it was one of the best seminars that I ever took in my life, and I am trying to share it with the people I am close to. I am much better with people now. I could even make a speech in front of a large audience now . . . maybe."

"Anything else?"

"Yeah, do more listening for a change."

"Okay."

* * * *

Debbie was waiting in front of Dairy Queen.

"Hi, Debbie. How are you doing?"

"Fine, and you?"

"Great. You ready to head over?"

"Sure."

"Debbie, I heard that Diane Wiest is really good in this movie. I'm not usually a big fan, but everyone says that she is just superb."

"Oh, I've always liked her," said Debbie. "I've seen all her movies."

"Oh." They reached the theatre, paid for their tickets separately, and went in.

"Let's get our seats first and then get something. Where do you like to sit usually, Debbie?"

"How about halfway up and on the end? I have to sit on the end because inevitably someone with a hat or big hair comes and sits right in front of me at the very last second when it's too dark to move. It's uncanny. How about here?"

They settled into their seats and removed their jackets. "Debbie, do you want popcorn or something to drink? My treat!" Julie asked as she half-climbed over Debbie's knees.

"Oh, thanks. Ummmm, 7-Up, or ginger ale if they don't have that. Medium. And how about we share a popcorn?"

"Okay, be right back."

Fortunately, it was a well-acted, engaging film, so it was easy for Julie to concentrate on it rather than being nervous and focusing only on Debbie. She did note at which scenes Debbie laughed and couldn't help but wonder why she laughed at those parts; they weren't that funny. That was incompatibility right there. In fact, it was kind of insensitive, almost vulgar of her to laugh in those parts. They stayed right to the end because you never knew what little treat awaited you at the end of the credits.

"That was great!" enthused Debbie as they put on their coats and stepped into the aisle. "She was soooo good. Oscar time! She's definitely going to get nominated. Great! Great! So, Starbucks?"

"Sure, that sounds great," replied Julie.

They walked outside and had taken about four steps when Debbie began to veer toward a telephone booth. "I have a quick call to make, okay?"

"Sure."

Julie lounged around the booth kicking at the sidewalk trying not to listen, but it wasn't a soundproof booth.

"Yes, Carmen. Mhmmm, right, right. Well, I *did* call you, but you never called me back . . . No, you didn't. I was there almost all day . . . No, no you didn't . . . You called the other line then." She rolled her eyes at

Julie through the glass. "Well, can we talk about it another time? I'm not alone right now . . . Julie . . . Julie Bell."

Things Julie wanted to do at that precise moment: throw a brick through the glass, reach in and slap Debbie; fall through the pavement; disappear on a space shuttle; become invisible, or become a bird and fly away, far, far away.

"What are you talking about? You got it last night . . . . What did you tell them? Not too much, I hope . . . The harness, why? What did you say? Oh, tell them that your pretty girlfriend might get jealous . . . Okay, okay. Love you too, sweetie . . . Yes, yes, I will . . . No, no, I won't . . . Right, I love you, too. Okay, bye, honey."

"Sorry about that," said Debbie as she slid open the door and stepped out.

"No problem."

"Now, where were we? Oh yes, Diane Wiest. Fabulous!"

* * * *

She wasn't expecting the call when it came. "Hello," said Julie disinterestedly.

"Julie," said Adrienne.

"Adrienne! Hi, how are you?"

"Could be better, and so could you."

"You've heard the latest, then."

"Of course I've heard. You should have waited, Julie. I told you that I would get back to you, and I meant it. That's why I left the message on your machine. What else do I have to do?"

"I called to apologize, really, sort of pre-impress you before you called back, and then it just escalated."

"Of course it escalated between you two. What did you expect? I am tired of all of this. I am not blaming anybody anymore. I am so tired of blame. Look, I said that I was going to meet you and I will, but until then, please don't call here anymore no matter what your intentions. It always causes trouble. I have lots of things to say that I didn't say to you in the mall. We need to talk more. I know that it's my fault, all of this."

"I've always wanted to talk."

"How about I pick you up around nine on Thursday night, and we can go for a drive?"

"Okay."

"Okay, nine, in front of your building."

"Okay, you remember where I live? Ha, ha, just kidding."

* * * *

Sarah took a sip of her iced jasmine tea and then said carefully, "Well, finally."

Sarah had acutely felt the seesaw for the last couple of months that had been torturing Julie. Adrienne should have let it happen months ago, but she hid. It was understandable, though. Most people want to hide. Adrienne wanted an easy way out of something that didn't have one. Sarah knew that Julie hated people telling her to get up and move on, but it was the crucial junction.

"Remember when you were talking about the disproportionate time thing, Julie? What you give her far exceeds what she gives you, and what you take is a fraction of what she gets from you. It's best that relationships be relatively equal, not like this. Don't let her do this anymore, Julie. She's not the only girl in the world. She's not. She's not the only thing to think about. Please don't be hurt or angry when I say that you're gonna have to accept that because I don't think you truly have yet."

"I know." Julie nodded and fiddled with her spoon, tapping it lightly onto the serviette and staining it a watery brown. "But who knows what she is going to say on this drive? I mean, we truly don't know other people's minds, Sarah. She could have had enough of Meagan already. Maybe Meagan beats her. She could say anything. She could . . . oh my god."

"What?" asked Sarah as she turned around to look at the door.

"Oh my god, it's Heather," moaned Julie. She put her hand to her forehead and rubbed her temples and shut her eyes. "What am I going to do?"

Heather only glanced at them as she passed and was now standing in front of the bookcase. She stood there for a couple of minutes with her head tilted, then picked out a book and sat at a table for two with her back to Julie.

"What's she doing, Sarah?" Julie whispered.

"Sitting down and reading. You mean you never returned even one of her calls?"

"She look over here?"

"No."

"Aw fuck, no, I didn't return her calls. She's gonna hate me. She knows I hang out here."

"It wouldn't hurt you to just go over there and say hi."

"Yes, it would. It would hurt very much. What's she doing?"

"Same, sitting and reading."

"Oh god, what timing. When it rains, it pours. What's she doing?"

"Taking out a gun."

Julie didn't join Sarah's laughter.

"Same thing, Julie. No wait. There's been a development, Ladies and Gentlemen. She's ordering! And it looks like flirting a bit, too. Exaggerated smile for the circumstances, that's for sure. She's cute. Do you remember if she's a good kisser?"

"Shut up."

"You going to avoid her forever? Come on. Don't hurt her feelings. She probably feels really bad. Once you confront the problem, you'll feel better. It's never as bad as you think, right?"

"You don't exactly confront your problems."

"That's irrelevant when it comes to giving advice to my friends. It's merely another one of your stalling tactics."

"Sometimes I'd really like to wring your neck."

Sarah laughed. "You gonna stop coming here? She's sitting down again. Just get it over with."

"Give me time to think a minute."

"Oooooh, look at her. Go over there and say hi. She looks so lonely. Make her feel better, Julie. Can't you do that? You know what it's like to feel so shitty. Everyone has been trying to cheer you up lately."

Julie resignedly pushed her chair away from the table, got up, and went over.

She touched Heather lightly on the arm. "Hi," she said.

Heather looked up from her book and smiled. "Hi."

"How are you?"

"Fine, and you?"

"Fine, well, not fine, but okay. Look, I'm sorry that I didn't call you back. I . . . I . . . was busy, and then I just forgot, and then this whole Adrienne thing..."

"It's okay. I can take a hint."

"It wasn't a hint. It was . . . well . . . ."

"It's okay. I'm used to it."

"Heather, don't . . . ."

"Look, you can justify it any way you want to, Julie. Call it a hint or not call it a hint. That's up to you. What I know is that if you really want to talk to someone, you will. If you really like someone, you will never be too busy to see her and will eventually make time for her no matter what. Always. Without exception. So could you just please spare me whatever excuses or reasons you have cooked up? Spare me, please. I'm not in the mood."

"Okay."

"You know, I can't stand making people feel obligated. I hate that. I would rather you didn't call at all then if you felt like that. I mean I didn't want to marry you or anything. I just wanted to maybe try some dating, have someone to go to a movie with, or have dinner and talk a bit, and after the party well, I thought it wasn't unreasonable. I thought that we'd get along. I am sorry. I didn't mean to appear desperate. I'm just lonely sometimes. That's all."

"I'm sorry. Please don't hate me."

"No, that's not right. That's the wrong word, Julie. I don't *hate* you. That's having something, and this is more what I don't have. It's an absence of good feelings anymore. It's an absence of thrill and anticipation of hearing from you. It's an absence of a smile when I think of you. There's a big difference between hating someone and not wanting to talk to them anymore. Don't flatter yourself that I waste my big emotions on you."

Julie felt ashamed and flustered, stripped of the capacity to respond.

"But everything is okay. I did enjoy myself at the party with you. I shouldn't have called so many times. I should have waited to hear from you. Demanding, impatient, and desperate are not exactly sexy. Anyway, you gave me a good memory. I've had many laughs over that one."

Julie tried to laugh, too. "Yes, that party definitely had its moments. Look, can we salvage that little bit of like and maybe get together for coffee sometime? I mean, well, how convenient. Here we are in a coffee shop! I don't mean now, but how about in the future?"

"It's okay, Julie. Actually, believe it or not, I have a date tonight. I'm just here early. I met a girl a couple of weeks ago."

"That's not hard to believe. That's great!" Julie was surprised by the tremor of jealousy that she suddenly felt. "Hey, do you want to meet my best friend Sarah for a minute? She was at the party. Do you remember her?"

"Not really . . . I mean, not really I don't remember, not really I don't want to meet her. Sure."

* * * *

"Kinda like one of our first dates," said Julie as she got in the car, "except in those days you looked a lot happier."

"Park, okay?"

"Sure."

It was this park in the middle of the city that they used to drive slowly through when they had first started seeing each other. They'd drive for hours talking and holding hands, not wanting to leave each other, not going home. Everything was interesting, profound, and precious. They'd pick up coffees from Tim Hortons and hold the steaming cups carefully between their legs as they drove around and around and around. Talk was so easy when they drove. They'd come along seemingly empty parked cars and look for the occupants in the back seat. Police cruisers would creep by them making them feel nervous. The bushes were dark and full, slightly menacing.

Sometimes they parked and looked out over the water. They watched the lights stretch out invitingly on the other side and got a little hypnotized by the night's power of transformation.

Julie asked, "You been out here recently?"

"Not recently."

Julie's nervousness had dissipated naturally in the familiar surroundings, though it was hard for her to reconcile being so emotionally far away from someone who was so familiar. She was hoping to prolong the chatting, hoping to delay the seriousness. It hadn't surfaced yet, but the flood was beginning to rise, and just below her skin Julie felt that Adrienne was not going to ask to come back. Did she know it? If she did, she wasn't ready to hear it. You had to be ready to hear it. You had to be ready for someone to tell you those kinds of things. That's why people suffered shock--because they weren't ready.

"I guess you've been pretty busy these days for drives and stuff," said Julie.

"Meagan's not much for driving."

Julie bristled at the sound of Meagan's name, but calmed down by telling herself that it was only natural that Adrienne would have to say the name. She had to pronounce it; she had to say Meagan. She couldn't just say 'the-woman-that-I-am-living-with-right-now doesn't like to drive.' Or 'the-fucking-conceited-no-talent-lousy-lover-bitch that I have saddled myself with' . . . Julie, Julie get a hold of yourself.

"Oh, I thought that she liked whipping around in that Explorer."

"She prefers road trips. She likes to drive where she can go fast. The city is too limiting."

What the hell. One last chance? Dive in, Julie.

"Of course. Well then, perhaps you two aren't as well-matched as you had thought. It starts with the little things as you well know."

Adrienne didn't pick it up. She said nothing, so Julie gushed to fill the silence.

"I am so sorry about the calls, Adrienne. I swear I don't remember the first one. It was a blackout. And the second one, well, I did intend to apologize, truly."

"I know you try, Julie. I know you mean well."

"Thanks for caring."

Julie reached over for Adrienne's hand, but Adrienne didn't offer it.

"Julie, don't."

Stung with embarrassment and hurt, Julie drew hers back and rested it in her lap.

"I just came out here to clear everything up, everything that we haven't said. I know how you hold onto things. The mall was a lousy choice before. I just want to say that I am so sorry. I have something to tell you."

Julie involuntarily held her breath. "Mmmhmm."

"I'm not with Meagan anymore. We broke up."

Julie didn't dare speak.

"We weren't good for each other."

Julie kept holding her breath because it was a firework moment. Though it was mere seconds, those seconds were an acute kaleidoscope of love, longing, confusion, and desperation that exploded into beautiful colours and patterns in her mind's sky, dazzling her.

"So, can we . . . ."

"No, Julie. It doesn't mean I am coming back to you. It's over."

A spark has fallen on Julie. It has burned and branded.

"I just came to tell you that I'm going away for a few months. I'm gonna work for my uncle in Winnipeg until Christmas. I need to get away from everything. It will help you, too. When I come back it will be a new beginning, a fresh start for all of us."

"Why did you and Meagan . . . ."

"Not now, Julie, please."

Julie kept her head bowed, her hands now together in her lap. She hadn't planned on trying to touch Adrienne, and she certainly hadn't planned on hearing anything like this. She had planned only two things: to forgive Adrienne and take her back, or to finally accept the rejection and accept it nobly. It wasn't exactly noble how her emotions overwhelmed and disobeyed her. They lured her and then betrayed her, ripped apart her intentions and dragged her where she hadn't planned. Oh, she knew that she had lost. She knew it. Her stomach was tight and pained and her head began pounding as her body accepted what her mind was trying to refuse.

Adrienne reached sideways and touched the back of Julie's neck, but for only a delicate, compensatory moment.

"I know how you think about things, Jules. You have to clear your mind of my details as much you can. We need this time apart so that we can be friends again one day in the future. I want to be friends. I am so sorry. I only hope that you will be able to understand someday." She was crying. "I am so sorry," she said. She wiped away tears with her hand and then brought it back to rest on the steering wheel.

"So this means that we're never going to get back together. Never? There's no chance? You won't change your mind? After you've recovered from Meagan?"

Adrienne whispered. "I'm so sorry."

Julie reached for the door handle. She half-opened the door and then stopped.

"Wait, I just want to ask you one thing."

"Yes, Julie, I did. Very much."

"That should be enough, then. Thank you, Adrienne." She got out of the car.

"Jules, you can't walk. Let me drive you."

"I've walked from here before."

"Julie, I don't want anything to happen to you."

"Nothing's going to happen. I've paid my dues the last few months, so I'm clear for a while. Take care and good luck." She closed the door and began to walk on the edge of the road.

Adrienne drove slowly beside her for a few minutes until a car came up behind and she had to speed up.

THE END

Printed in the United States
110542LV00010B/13-42/P